AN ALL-CONSUMING PASSION

Morgan Kane's arrival on the beautiful Caribbean island was guaranteed to upset Holly's peaceful world, and she was determined to fight him for her freedom. But things didn't go according to her plan, at all . . .

AN
ALL-CONSUMING
PASSION

BY

ANNE MATHER

MILLS & BOON LIMITED
15–16 BROOK'S MEWS
LONDON W1A 1DR

First published in Great Britain 1985
by Mills & Boon Limited

© Anne Mather 1985

Australian copyright 1985
Philippine copyright 1986
This edition 1986

ISBN 0 263 75279 8

Set in Monophoto Times 10 on 11 pt.
01–0286 – 54678

Made and printed in Great Britain by
Richard Clay (The Chaucer Press) Ltd,
Bungay, Suffolk

CHAPTER ONE

'WE'LL be landing in less than fifteen minutes, Mr Kane.'

The pilot had turned from the controls to address his only passenger, and Morgan lifted his head from the papers he had been studying since they left St Thomas to meet the man's candid gaze.

'Fifteen minutes,' he echoed, his attractive voice low and well modulated. 'Okay, Joe. Thanks.'

'My pleasure, Mr Kane,' responded the dark-skinned pilot, resuming his appraisal of the instruments in front of him. 'Should still be light enough for you to see the island, if the weather holds up. Looks like that storm they promised us isn't going to show.'

Morgan hesitated a moment, cast a faintly regretful glance at the documents he had taken from the briefcase beside him, and then came to a decision. Sliding the papers back into their file, he pushed the file into the briefcase, snapping the fasteners shut before asking politely, 'Do you get a lot of storms here?'

'Hell, no!' Joe allowed a chuckle to escape him. 'Didn't Mr Forsyth tell you? Pulpit Island has an almost perfect climate. Little rain; plenty of sun; and the trades, to keep the temperature just bearable.'

Morgan acknowledged his ignorance. 'No hurricanes?' he enquired mildly, easing the collar of his shirt away from his neck, and Joe cast him a reproving grimace.

'Not since 1973,' he asserted. 'Like I said, you're going to love it here, Mr Kane.'

'I don't think I'll be here long enough to form an

opinion,' remarked Morgan drily, looking down on to a sea as clear and blue-green as aquamarines. 'Is that Pulpit Island down there?'

'No, sir, that's Little Orchis,' said Joe, tipping the plane's wing so that they turned in a south-easterly direction. 'You'll be able to see Pulpit Island any minute now. Would you like me to give you an aerial tour before we land?'

'I don't think that will be necessary,' said Morgan smoothly. 'Where do we land? In the harbour?'

'Oh, the old sweet pea splashes down in Charlotte's Bay,' answered Joe, with another chuckle, patting the controls of the vintage seaplane, which plied its trade in island-hopping. 'Mighty handy as it turns out. The old Gantry place is right on the bay. That way Miss Holly knows the minute her father reaches the island.'

Morgan propped his chin on one lean brown hand and gazed a little ruefully out of the window. He hoped Holly had had her father's telegram. It would make things infinitely more difficult if she was not anticipating his arrival. Besides which, she would have had no warning of what her father wanted her to do.

Shifting his long legs a little impatiently, he wished, not for the first time, that Andrew hadn't involved him in his private affairs. It was one thing to be Andrew Forsyth's personal assistant, to know as much, if not more, than his employer about the day-to-day running of the Forsyth corporation, and to participate in the expansion of his business empire. It was quite another to be expected to persuade his twenty-year-old daughter—and only offspring—to return to London at her father's whim, when she must know as well as he did that there had to be more to it than her father's sudden desire to resume a paternal role.

It was too late now to try and pretend her father had any real affection for her. From the day she was born—

and Morgan could remember that day very well—she had been an unwanted encumbrance to him, a constant reminder of her mother, whose life had been forfeit to secure her own, and for which Andrew Forsyth had never forgiven her.

Morgan had not been Andrew's assistant then, of course. He had been a new, and very junior, executive, fresh out of university, with a double first in law and economics, and little else. It had been his first day with the company, and the personal affairs of his boss had seemed very distant indeed.

However, twenty years had seen a great number of changes. In time, his shrewdness in business and his capacity for hard work had been recognised, and by the time he joined Andrew's immediate staff, Holly Forsyth was no longer so remote from him. Not that he knew her well. A series of nannies, followed by a spell at an exclusive preparatory school, had made way for an equally exclusive boarding school, and if there had been problems, he had not been expected to handle them. Indeed, the first time he actually saw Holly in the flesh had been less than five years ago, when Andrew had asked him to pick her up from a friend's house in Woking and drive her to London airport to catch a plane for Zurich. And then, what with her non-communicativeness and the chauffeur's watching presence, they had scarcely exchanged more than a few words. He had thought at first that she was shy and, having children of his own now, he had done his utmost to put her at her ease. But the cool indigo eyes, watching his efforts from between narrowed lids, had had more than a touch of scorn in their depths, and he had quickly realised that Holly Forsyth knew exactly what he was trying to do.

Since then, his glimpses of her had been equally brief. Once, in London, soon after her return from the finishing school for which she had been sent to Switzerland, he had encountered her leaving her father's office, but on that occasion she had looked straight through him. He had suspected at the time that her over-bright eyes and flushed cheeks had mirrored an inner tumult, and certainly Andrew's temper had been decidedly unpredictable for the rest of the day. But then, he had learned, Andrew was always unpredictable where Holly was concerned, and Morgan doubted that anything she did would find approval with her father.

The last time he had laid eyes on her had been two years ago, just before she left England. He had called at Andrew's house in Hampstead late one evening to deliver some papers his employer had left at the office, and he had met Holly arriving home with a crowd of noisy young people. They were all high, whether on drink or marijuana, or perhaps a combination of both, Morgan couldn't be sure, and the row that had ensued when Andrew erupted from his study had not been pleasant.

Morgan had not wanted to get involved, but it was Holly herself who had involved him. With artless provocation, she had slipped her arm through his and compelled him to stay, using his strength to support her when her father's wrath washed over her. A tall girl, with cropped fair hair and a slim, still adolescently angular body, she had faced her father bravely, unaware that Andrew Forsyth wasn't even listening to her. Poor Holly, Morgan remembered now, the colour leaving her face so quickly that the expertly used cosmetics became as conspicuous as a clown's mask. She should have known better than to try and fight Andrew Forsyth. Men with far fewer scruples had tried and failed, and Holly simply did not have the weapons.

If only she had not looked so much like her mother, perhaps then her father might have been able to forget. But, having seen photographs of the first Mrs Forsyth, Morgan knew exactly why his employer found his daughter's presence so intolerable. Holly's mother was the only woman he had ever loved, and although there had been three other wives since her death, there had been no other children—not even a son to step into his father's shoes.

Unfortunately, Morgan had been able to do nothing to help her and, when she realised this, Holly had turned on him, too. As her friends drifted away in twos and threes, unable—or unwilling—to be a party to her humiliation, Andrew had delivered his final ultimatum. If she wanted him to go on supporting her, she would have to give up mixing with that crowd of queers and layabouts, or she could get out.

Six weeks later, Morgan heard that she had left for her mother's old home on Pulpit Island, one hundred and fifty miles from St Thomas in the Virgin Islands. Sara Gantry, Holly's mother, had been born in the West Indies, and her family had once owned a thriving sugar plantation there. But, what with the price of sugar falling and labour becoming increasingly expensive, the estate had largely been dismantled, even before Holly's grandparents died. However, the house was still standing and, according to Andrew, Holly had always been happy there.

'She used to go out for holidays, when she was younger,' he told Morgan, with a rare flash of what might have been conscience. 'She likes swimming and fishing, and messing about with crayons and water colours,' he added, when his assistant made no immediate comment. 'Don't judge me, Morgan. She always has been a thorn in my side.'

And who was he to judge anyway, reflected Morgan

drily, resting one booted ankle across his knee. His own sixteen-year-old twins were proving to be just as much of a liability, and how could he blame Andrew for ignoring his daughter when he spent so little time with his sons? According to Alison, his ex-wife, he was totally responsible for their delinquency and, in all honesty, he had been away a lot when they were growing up. Andrew was a demanding employer and, as his empire stretched from one side of the financial world to the other, Morgan had often been in Hong Kong or San Francisco when he should have been at home.

But had he been entirely to blame? To begin with, Alison had been delighted when, soon after their marriage, Morgan had been recruited to Andrew Forsyth's office. She had even encouraged him to make himself indispensable to his superior, and she had soon found uses for the higher salary his promotion had brought.

She had not wanted the twins, but their arrival less than two years after their marriage had coincided with their removal to a bigger flat, and she had been placated by the chance to prove her home-making abilities. Besides, she had discovered that having twins set her apart from other young mothers, who had only had one child at a time, and for a while she was content to bask in their reflected glory.

By the time the twins were two, however, motherhood had begun to pall, and Alison was clamouring for a garden to get them out of her hair. She didn't care that, to buy the house in Willesden, Morgan had to work a twelve-hour day. She had chosen it because it was near her mother's house, and in no time at all Mrs Stevens was caring for the twins while Alison spent her time in boutiques and beauty parlours.

But, eventually, even the novelty of an unlimited

supply of money did not satisfy her. Morgan's promotion to Andrew Forsyth's personal assistant meant that he and his wife were occasionally invited to dinner in Hampstead, and before long Alison was resentful of their own 'poky' domain. She saw no reason why they should not have a large house, *and* a housekeeper, now that Morgan had a position of authority.

They moved again, this time to a sprawling house in Wimbledon, with every accoutrement Alison could wish for. Five bedrooms, three bathrooms; there was even a sauna in the basement. It was the kind of luxury home anyone would be proud of. Only, now, boredom took the place of envy, and resentment of Morgan's more exciting lifestyle became the most contentious issue in Alison's life.

Morgan was unable to appease her. Her constant jibes and recriminations made life pretty difficult at times, and before long the twins began to notice. Salving his conscience with the conviction that the boys would be happier if they were not constantly witness to their parents' rows, Morgan had suggested boarding school. But for once Alison had demurred from taking the easy option.

'You'd like that, wouldn't you?' she had shouted, her fashionably thin features contorted into their habitual expression of dissatisfaction. 'Then you wouldn't need to feel any sense of guilt in neglecting your family, would you? You could go off with Andrew bloody Forsyth with a clear conscience!'

Morgan had endeavoured to explain that were he to resign his position as Andrew's assistant, they could not afford their present standard of living, but she had not listened. So far as his wife was concerned, he was a careless, selfish bastard, whose only real enjoyment was in making money for someone else.

Alison, meanwhile, was finding different pursuits. Abandoning any pretence of fidelity, she began to look for diversion in other quarters, and their relationship quickly foundered.

Yet, even then, she had fought their inevitable separation. Blaming Morgan yet again for his selfishness and neglect, she had fought for, and gained, custody of the two boys, and Morgan found himself faced with the upkeep of two households, instead of just one. Of course, the modest flat he occupied in Kensington did not stretch his income, but fighting Alison's influence on the twins was quite another matter.

Naturally, having been raised in such an atmosphere, they had been affected by it. Just in a small way at first: fighting in the playground, stealing small amounts of money from their mother's purse, getting such poor grades in school that the headmaster had called their father in for a discussion. But gradually, as they had grown older, their crimes had become more serious. When they were sent to the local comprehensive school, they frequently played truant, and when Morgan found out and paid for their transfer to a fee-paying boys' school, they were soon threatened with expulsion for using foul language. And finally, just recently, within weeks of leaving yet another fee-paying establishment, they had been caught shoplifting with some other boys in Oxford Street, and only the intervention of Andrew's lawyer had prevented them from a serious conviction.

It had not been an opportune moment for Andrew to ask Morgan to fly out to the West Indies to bring his daughter back to London. With the twins out of school and resentful of the restrictions he had persuaded Alison to put upon them, he had been loath to leave the country. But Andrew had had the solution.

'I'll speak to the commanding officer of the *Admiral Nelson*,' he declared, mentioning the name of a famous sailing vessel, used as a training ground for would-be naval recruits. 'Fawcett—that's the chap—he's a friend of mine, and if he can fit them into his schedule, he will. Three weeks living in pretty austere surroundings is exactly what they need, and they'll learn the rudiments of sailing as well as learning to work with other people as a team.'

'And do you think Jeff and Jon will comply?' asked Morgan doubtfully. 'Will Alison let them go?'

'If I ask her,' returned Andrew smugly, exchanging an amused smile with his assistant. 'It will do them a power of good. And it will get them away from their mother for a while, which can't be bad.'

Morgan shifted rather impatiently in his seat now and Joe, attracted by the movement, glanced round. 'That's Pulpit Island, Mr Kane,' he said, pointing down towards a mass of greenery, which seemed to be floating on the water. 'See that sickle curve of beach? That's Charlotte's Bay that it's wrapped around.'

'Oh—thanks.'

Morgan produced a smile and determinedly forced his mind to dwell on less disturbing things. As the plane banked to facilitate its approach he was able to discern the distinctive outcropping of rock, which Andrew had told him had given the island its name, rising over a thousand feet from the central highlands. The rest of the island appeared to be covered in a thriving mass of vegetation, a darkly tinted emerald, set in a frame of creamy white coral.

The island was bigger than he had expected, though as the seaplane plunged towards the enveloping curve of Charlotte's Bay, he could see little sign of life. 'Charlottesville—that's the capital—it's at the other side of the island,' the pilot commented, as if reading Morgan's thoughts. 'Not much of a capital, really. Just a handful of shops and warehouses, and a market that sells fruit and fish.'

Morgan wanted to reply, but the sea seemed to be hurtling up towards them at a terrifying pace. He felt the rush of adrenalin through his veins turn his stomach over, and he gripped the arms of his seat as the aircraft hit the water. *'Christ,'* he muttered weakly, as the plane's floats tore a channel across the bay, and a salty spray forced its way through a ventilator. Taking off had been slow, but landing certainly wasn't.

'You all right, Mr Kane?' asked Joe with some concern, as the aircraft slowed to a more sedate pace and chugged happily towards the shore. 'Guess you've never flown in the "goose" before, but you can rely on her. Safest transport around.'

'Is it?'

Morgan's tone was dry, but he couldn't help it. It had been a long day. First the nine-hour flight to Miami, then the forty-minute wait for his connection to St Thomas. And now this crazy island-hopping amphibian, which even now was having its wheels cranked down by hand so that, when they reached the shallows, it could waddle out on to the beach.

He glanced at his watch. It was almost half past six local time, but his body told him it was much later. Apart from which, he had an ache in his spine through sitting so long, and the alarm he had experienced on landing had covered his whole body in an unpleasant wave of heat.

Reaching up, he loosened his tie and peered somewhat wearily out of the window. Although it was early evening, the warmth now that the plane had landed was almost palpable, and he looked down at his dark grey three-piece suit with some impatience. He should have changed at Miami, he reflected. He had had time. But he had also needed a drink, and he hadn't had time for both.

The seaplane bumped up on to sand filtered from

successive generations of coral, washed by the lucid green waters of Charlotte's Bay. Ahead of the plane, the virginal white sand gave way to coconut groves and waving palms, and beyond that to the tangled forest he had seen from the air.

There was a boy standing on the beach, apparently waiting for the plane, and Joe waved to him, evidently recognising a friend. 'That's Samuel, Miss Holly's houseboy,' he explained to his passenger. 'Seems like she knew you were coming.'

'Seems like she did,' murmured Morgan drily, loosening his seat belt and automatically checking the zipper of his trousers. 'I *wonder*,' he added, under his breath, and when the plane halted, he got gratefully to his feet.

Because of his height, it was impossible to stand straight inside the plane, but Joe was already out of his seat, loosening the catches and thrusting open the door. He let Morgan precede him, standing back while the other man bent to negotiate the low lintel.

Morgan stepped down on to the sand that crunched beneath the soles of his shoes, and into a wave of heat infinitely more enervating than the cloistered atmosphere on board had been. The seaplane had kept reasonably cool throughout the flight, and the wash of water against its hull had kept it cool on landing. But outside, in the still powerful rays of the setting sun, the temperature was considerably higher, and the jacket of his suit felt damp beneath his arms.

With a gesture of impatience, he shrugged out of the offending garment and slung it over one shoulder, aware of the amused gaze of the boy on the beach as he took in the equally uncomfortable waistcoat beneath. Samuel—if that was his name—was wearing sawn-off jeans and a flapping T-shirt, and his dark, bronzed skin gleamed dully with the patina of good health. He

was perhaps sixteen, Morgan estimated, the twins' age.
But he was taller than they were, and not so stocky, his
long legs protruding from the knee-length denims.

'Mr Kane?' he enquired, stepping forward, his
expression sobering abruptly. 'Miss Forsyth sent me
to meet you. She's waiting for you back at the house.'

'Oh, thanks.' Morgan inclined his head in acknowledgment, as Joe hoisted his overnight-case out of the
plane. He shrugged. 'Is it far to the house?'

'Hell, no. That's it—over there,' exclaimed Joe, pre-
empting the boy's response. He pointed a long finger,
and Morgan squinted into the deepening gloom. The
sun was sinking fast, and the island was bathed in an
amber radiance, an almost unholy glow that was
rapidly turning to umber.

The Forsyth house seemed to stand on a rise,
overlooking the bay. A white, verandahed portico was
overset with dark iron-railed balconies and, even from
this distance, Morgan could see the profusion of plant-
life growing all around it. It was bigger than he had
expected, and many of the windows were shuttered, but
a light was glowing from a downstairs window
revealing Holly's occupancy.

'Let's go,' said Samuel, apparently resenting Joe's
interference in what he considered to be his territory.
He picked up Morgan's suitcase and took a few pointed
steps along the beach. 'You coming, Mr Kane?'

'Er—yes. Yes, of course.' Morgan dragged his eyes
away from the house and turned briefly back to the
pilot. 'Thanks,' he said, shaking the man's hand.
'Now—how do I get in touch with you when I want to
go back?'

'Miss Holly'll arrange all that,' responded Joe, with a
grin. 'You have a good holiday now. You hear?'

Morgan forbore from repeating that this was not a
holiday, and grinned in return. 'Okay,' he said. 'See you

soon.' And, with a final gesture of farewell, he started after Samuel's lanky form.

By the time they had reached the stretch of beach below the house, the seaplane had shimmied back into the water and was making its take-off. The roar of its engines was an ugly intrusion into a stillness disturbed only by the piping sound of the crickets, and a flock of birds rose protestingly from their nesting place, startled by the unaccustomed violation of their privacy.

Samuel balanced Morgan's suitcase on his head, holding it steady with one hand, as they left the beach to climb a shallow flight of steps to the house. There must have been fifty of them, Morgan decided, feeling the constriction in his chest as he followed Samuel's unhurried tread. It made him realise that a weekly work-out at the squash club was not a total compensation for a sedentary life, and he was panting pretty badly by the time they reached the top.

It was fully dark now, but the air was fragrant with the scent of night-blooming plants and delicate honeysuckle. They picked their way across a garden that had evidently been left to go to seed, and brushed between a mass of statuary before climbing two more steps to a lawned area in front of the house. The lights from the house gave more illumination here, revealing that the grass had, at least, been cut, and the borders trimmed. An old cane chair reclined in the shade of a flowering acacia, and on the verandah a pair of cushioned sun-loungers were set beside a basket-woven table.

It wasn't until they were actually climbing the steps up to the verandah that Morgan realised someone was standing there, in the darkness, watching their approach. She had not occupied either of the sun-loungers that flanked the circular table, where a jug of iced cordial drew his thirsty gaze. She was standing in the shadows, against the wall of the building, and she only moved into the light when she was obliged to do so.

Even then, Morgan had some difficulty in relating this golden-skinned creature to the Holly Forsyth he remembered. Setting down his briefcase, he ran a hand around the back of his neck, flinching from the dampness of his skin. He was sweating quite profusely now, and it didn't help to be confronted by someone as cool and self-possessed as this young woman seemed to be.

Although the skinny vest and skimpy shorts she was wearing in no way compared to the expensive suits and dresses her father had bought her, Holly had an air of elegance all her own. It was something to do with the way she moved, a natural co-ordination that had not been in evidence the last time they had met. She was still slim, but her bones were less obviously visible and, although he had not intended to look, he couldn't help his awareness of breasts fuller and firmer than when he had last seen her in England. She had let her hair grow, too, and it now hung a couple of inches below her shoulders, smooth and silky, and bleached several shades lighter by the sun. It was odd, he thought inconsequently, that sun lightened the hair but darkened the flesh. And because Holly was wearing no make-up, her skin had the lustre of good health.

'Hello, Mr Kane,' she said now, holding out her hand. 'Did you have a good trip?' and Morgan dried his palm down the seam of his trousers before accepting her polite salutation.

'It's good to be here,' he acknowledged, threading long fingers into the clinging dampness of his hair. 'I feel like I've been trapped in a steel girdle for the past twelve hours.' He grinned. 'I guess I'm getting too old to sit still for so long. My spine feels like it's been kicked by a mule.'

Holly's lips parted to reveal even white teeth. 'You're not old, Mr Kane,' she said, her eyes frankly admiring, and as Morgan's stomach twisted, she added, 'Now—which would you like first? A drink or a shower?'

Morgan took a deep breath. 'Would I be rude if I said both?' he queried drily, deciding he had imagined that provocative glance. 'Something long and cool would be just perfect. And then I'd like to get out of these unsuitable clothes.'

'Of course.' Holly turned to Samuel then, and directed him to take Mr Kane's bags to his room. As the boy rescued Morgan's briefcase and departed, she appended, 'You don't appear to have brought very much. But that's just as well, because we don't go in for formality around here.'

Morgan gestured to a chair, too weary right now to go into the details of why he had brought so few clothes, and Holly nodded. 'Oh—please,' she said, moving to the table and picking up the frosted jug. 'I hope you like daiquiris. I asked Lucinda to prepare these earlier.'

Morgan sank gratefully on to the cushioned sun-lounger and arched one dark brow. 'Lucinda?'

'Samuel's mother,' explained Holly, as the chink of ice clunked satisfyingly into a glass. 'She and Micah—that's her husband—and Samuel, of course, are all the staff there are here now.'

Morgan rested his head back against the cushions, allowing an unaccustomed feeling of peace to envelop him. He didn't know why exactly, but he was relaxing for the first time in days and, in spite of the fact that this was not a holiday, he knew an unexpected sense of well-being.

Of course, it might have something to do with the fact that he knew Alison could not reach him here. In spite of the divorce, which had severed all formal connections between them, she still played a considerable part in his life, and it was a relief to be free of her continued complaints. With the twins having a constant claim to his affections, there was little he could do to escape her demands, unless he was prepared to risk their alienation, too. Living with their mother, they were prone to take her side in any argument, and Morgan knew Alison lost no opportunity of blaming their father for the break-up of the marriage. Even this trip to the Caribbean had not met with her approval, even though she had accepted Andrew's plans for the boys without demur.

'Why can't the girl simply get on a plane by herself?' she had exclaimed, when Morgan had told her what he intended to do. 'She's not a child, is she? From what I hear, she's hardly an innocent!'

'Did you tell Andrew that?' enquired Morgan drily, retaliating with more cynicism than usual, and even over the phone he heard her sudden intake of breath.

'Don't bait me, Morgan,' she retorted fiercely, and he could sense the cold resentment she still felt for the security of his position. She had always been jealous of his friendship with Andrew, and not even the prospect of destroying her own lifestyle had prevented her from trying to lose Morgan his job when he first moved out of the house. 'Just because you would do anything that man asked you, doesn't mean that I can't have my own opinion of the Forsyths. Just don't imagine Andrew would let you anywhere near his precious daughter! He may have no time for her himself, but I'm sure he appreciates the potential she offers!'

Her words had at last got under Morgan's skin, and his gritted response revealed the fact. 'She's twenty years old, Alison,' he had told her, his voice harsh with contempt. 'She's young enough to be my *daughter*! For Christ's sake, what do you take me for?'

Morgan thrust these thoughts aside now as Holly

came to hand him a tall glass. He had known Alison was just taking out her spite on him, but he had been furious that she could still penetrate his defences. Of course, she still resented the fact that physically she no longer attracted him. She had thought that, in spite of her infidelities, Morgan would continue to want her body, but he hadn't. The discovery that she had been sleeping with other men while he had been away had destroyed any feelings Morgan had still had for her, and since their separation he had satisfied his needs elsewhere.

'Is it all right?'

Holly's query caused him to look up at her ruefully, raising his glass to his lips as he did so. 'Very good,' he said, somewhat hoarsely moments later, as the raw spirit caught his dry throat. 'But I think—Lucinda, did you say—has a heavy hand with the rum. Do you always drink them this potent?'

Holly laughed, a low musical sound that was entirely feminine, and seated herself on the sun-lounger beside him. To do so, she swung one leg across the cushioned footrest, giving him a revealing glimpse of her inner thigh as she did so, before scooping both knees up in front of her and circling them with her arms. 'Oh—I don't drink them,' she assured him, her oval features alight with amusement. 'Besides, I'm not thirsty right now. I just had a shower.'

'An inviting prospect,' remarked Morgan wryly, swallowing a generous portion of the liquid in his glass as thirst got the better of discretion. 'But much more of this and I won't be able to see the shower, let alone the taps.'

'Would you prefer a beer?' asked Holly innocently, glancing towards the house, but Morgan shook his head.

'This is fine, for now,' he responded, his tongue

circling his lips. 'So—tell me: did you get your father's telegram?' He paused. 'You do know why I'm here?'

'Let's not talk business on your first evening,' Holly answered lightly, swinging her legs to the slatted boards of the verandah once again. 'Come on. I'll show you your room. Are you hungry? I told Lucinda just to prepare something light for supper.'

Morgan hesitated, but then, after finishing the daiquiri, he got obediently to his feet. She was right. They'd have plenty of time tomorrow to discuss her father's invitation, and the alcohol had left him feeling pleasantly lethargic.

Holly led the way through a meshed door into the entrance hall of the house. A wide, high-ceilinged area, with fluted columns supporting a galleried landing, and solid blocks of squared marble underfoot, it was an impressive, if slightly time-worn, introduction to the building. But the wall-lights, screened by copper shades, which illuminated the faded beauty of the house, also illuminated Holly's features, and Morgan's attention was arrested. On the verandah, she had been extremely attractive; in the lamplight, she was quite startlingly beautiful, her long indigo eyes and delicately moulded cheekbones giving character to a wide and mobile mouth. Christ, he chided himself, giving in to a totally uncharacteristic criticism of his employer's methods. No wonder Andrew thought she might have something to offer. In shabby beach clothes she was a naiad; in designer fashions she would be magnificent.

'Is something wrong?'

The dark indigo eyes were upon him, and to his embarrassment, Morgan felt the seep of hot colour under his skin. 'No,' he said abruptly. 'No, I was just— admiring my surroundings. The building seems extremely old. Is it the original plantation house?'

'Heavens, no. That was burned down years ago,'

replied Holly after a moment. 'My great-grandfather had this place built around the turn of the century. It's much more modest than the old house. Or so my grandfather used to tell me.'

'Really?'

Morgan tried to keep his attention on the building as he followed Holly up the stairs. The staircase curved round a ninety-degree angle before reaching the gallery above, the wooden steps worn in places, but still lovingly varnished. There were pictures lining the wall, and it was a relief to look at them and not at Holly's only slightly swaying hips, nor at the long brown legs that emerged from the hem of her shorts, or the narrow bare feet that strode ahead of him. Far better to admire the distinctive curve of Charlotte's Bay at sunset, an image still firmly imprinted on his thoughts. Or the tangled glory of a neglected garden which, although he had not seen it clearly, looked suspiciously like the one below the house.

'Did you do these?' he asked at last, remembering Andrew's careless mention of an artistic temperament, and Holly paused.

'Yes,' she said, without affectation. 'Do you like them? They're not much good, but as my father would say, they keep me occupied.'

Morgan shook his head. 'But they are good,' he contradicted her incredulously. 'I'm no expert, but I have attended auctions, and believe me, you evidently have a talent.'

Holly grimaced. 'Hmm.' She shook her head and then continued on her way. 'I doubt if my father would agree with you. So far as he's concerned, women are good for one thing only.' She cast him a faintly mocking glance. 'Wouldn't you say?'

Morgan's mouth drew down at the corners. 'I doubt if you have proof of that,' he commented drily, but Holly's gaze did not falter.

'He has had four wives,' she reminded him, with disturbing candour. 'And I can't believe he married them for their conversation.'

Morgan wished he'd never started this, but before he could change the subject Holly had halted outside a cream, panelled door. 'Your room,' she said, turning the handle and pushing the door open. Then, preceding him into the room, she switched on a lamp by the bed. 'It's my father's,' she added carelessly. 'I didn't see any point in having Lucinda air another room.'

Morgan looked about him with guarded interest. The room was huge and rather spartanly furnished. It was dominated by the massive square four-poster that occupied the central area, but apart from the bed and its sombre velvet tester, there was no sign of the luxury Andrew enjoyed at his house in England. There was a chest of drawers with a mirror above; a walk-in wardrobe; an ottoman, on which resided his suitcase; and a leather-topped table by the window, which could serve a dual purpose as a desk. The floor was bare, just polished wooden boards, with a plain skin rug beside the bed to add a little colour.

'The bathroom's through there,' said Holly indicating a door, 'but I'm afraid you'll have to share with me. As you'll find out, the Fletchers and I only occupy a small part of the house. The rest is shuttered—closed off—to save unnecessary labour, you see.'

Morgan inclined his head. 'I understand.'

'So . . .' Holly lifted her slim shoulders and then let them fall again. 'If you need anything else, just holler, as Samuel would say. Supper will be ready in about an hour. Unless you'd like it sooner.'

'An hour will be just fine,' Morgan assured her firmly, loosening the remaining buttons of his waistcoat and stripping it off. Then, without thinking, he pulled off his tie and started to unfasten his shirt, only realising she was still hovering in the doorway when he looked up and met her gaze.

'I don't suppose your wife wanted you to come, did she?' Holly murmured, smoothing the edge of the door with her fingers, and the unexpectedly personal quality of her question caught him unprepared.

'I—my wife and I are divorced,' he said shortly, his hands stilling as he became aware of a disturbing change in their relationship. In the past he had always regarded her as a child, not much older than the twins in fact, and definitely not someone he would speak to as an equal. But now that was all changed. Now she was speaking to him as a woman. And, in spite of himself, Morgan felt his senses stir at the thinly veiled insolence of her regard.

'I see,' remarked Holly softly, apparently not at all dismayed by his shocked reaction. 'I can't say I'm surprised.'

And, with a lazy smile, she withdrew, closing the door behind her and leaving Morgan to stare blankly at the worn cream panels.

CHAPTER TWO

THE sun had barely cleared the trees on the other side of the island when Holly slid out of bed. It wasn't much after six, but she had been awake for hours, watching the curtains moving in the breeze from her balcony, and going over the previous evening's events and her own reaction to them.

Now, however, she could lie still no longer. Thrusting back the covers, she strode eagerly across the floor, halting only reluctantly when her slim naked form was reflected in the mirrors of her dressing-table. She could hardly step out on to the balcony without any clothes, however attractive that proposition might be, she reflected. With a sigh of resignation, she caught up a shred of pure white satin that resolved itself into a simple wrapper and, tying the cord about her waist, she followed her inclination.

Outside the air was magic, a mixture of tangy salt and the blossoming bougainvillaea that rioted over the roof of the verandah below. The view, too, was matchless: an arc of blue-green water, caught in the arms of a verdant lover—twin headlands curving round to cradle the sheltered bay. Below the house, the beach was clean and untouched, the footprints left by her visitor washed away by the morning tide. Nearer at hand, bees already buzzed among the tangled mass of flowers, and Micah had set a sprinkler going to moisten the sun-scorched grass.

Resting her arms on the balcony rail, Holly breathed deeply, allowing the beauty of the day to dispel the sense of anxiety that had disturbed her sleep since her father's telegram had arrived. He could not force her to go back, she told herself fiercely, wondering if she really believed that by saying something often enough one could make it happen. He hadn't even had the decency to come and ask her himself—albeit that her answer would still have been the same. He had sent Morgan Kane: his mentor, his *alter ego*; the man Holly hated most in the world.

She breathed a little more quickly when she thought about what she was going to do to Morgan Kane. It was strange but, until two years ago, he had been the man she most admired. Not that he had been aware of it, of course. To him, she was just a child, Andrew Forsyth's unwanted daughter, the metaphorical cross his employer had to bear. She had known that, and accepted it, too long used to being treated as a pariah in her father's household to find anything unusual in being ignored.

Yet there had been times when Morgan had not ignored her, times when she had thought he was doing his best to compensate for her father's negligence. To begin with, she had not trusted his overtures of friendship, assuming her father had told him exactly what to say. But, gradually, as her love-starved young body began to mature, she had started to see Morgan in an entirely different light. She had actually begun to believe he cared about her.

Her trust had been abruptly shattered one night, a little over two years ago. She had turned to Morgan for help, and he had not given it. Instead, he had taken her father's part in humiliating her in front of her friends. He had not even tried to defend her actions. He had shown himself for the cipher he was, and she knew she had been a fool ever to have believed it could be otherwise.

After that, for a spell, she had not cared what

happened to her. Because of what had happened she lost touch with the group of young people she had been running around with, and she wasn't exactly sorry. She had known they were a wild bunch, and that sooner or later they were going to get caught. But she missed their cheerful companionship, and the sometimes crazy things they used to do.

The suggestion she had made of going to art school in Paris had seemed like a good idea at the time, but once again her father had denied it. No daughter of his was going to waste her time daubing colours on paper, he said, though they both knew it wasn't just the occupation that appalled him. He didn't want her to be happy. He had made that blatantly plain. He only wanted to be rid of her, and her suggestion of coming here had suited him very well.

Pulpit Island. Holly sighed now, wondering rather bitterly whether Andrew Forsyth would have let her come here had he known she would not miss her life in England. She suspected he saw her confinement as a kind of punishment, but in fact they had been the happiest two years of her life.

She had always been happy here. When she was a child, her dearest memories had been of holidays spent on Pulpit Island with her grandparents. It was the one place where she had been accepted for herself, and not as her father's daughter, and her mother's parents had never blamed her for being the cause of their daughter's death. Their deaths, soon after one another, when she was in her early teens, had left a void in her life, a void, she now realised, she had imagined Morgan Kane might fill. But he hadn't. He had abandoned her just when she needed him most, and for that she could never forgive him.

It was not something she had brooded about over these past two years. Indeed, apart from the painful bitterness she had brought with her to the island, she had eventually succeeded in putting all thoughts of him out of her head. But when she got her father's telegram, when she learned he was sending Morgan Kane to do his dirty work once again, her spirit had rebelled. She was a good-looking young woman, she knew that without any trace of conceit, and she also knew she was attractive to men. Even here, on Pulpit Island, where most of the men she met were either old or married, she was not unaware of her popularity, and it had come to her in a flash that she might be able to hurt both Morgan and her father. How furious Andrew Forsyth would be if his blameless personal assistant blotted his copy-book! Holly thought maliciously. And how delicious her revenge if she could make him forget his responsibilities.

She frowned momentarily as reason reared its ugly head. She suspected she was being overly romantic in imagining she could persuade a man like Morgan Kane to actually fall in love with her. He was so much older, after all, and obviously more experienced. Besides which, he had spent the last fifteen years visiting the most sophisticated capitals of the world and, although he had been married then, he had probably known lots of other women. He was an attractive man; more attractive than she remembered, she acknowledged ruefully, nibbling her thumb. Or perhaps she was looking at him differently now, knowing what was in her mind. It was a pity he was divorced, but that could not be helped. Her father would still be furious if Morgan made a fool of him.

Now, she cast a reflective glance along the balcony. Her father's room—the room Morgan was occupying—opened on to this balcony, too. But there was no sign of life from his room as yet. The french doors were almost closed, and only the hem of the curtain, flapping in the breeze, gave any evidence that it was occupied.

Which was just as well, she decided, turning back into her bedroom. She wanted to have her swim, her breakfast, and be gone before he woke up. It would have been interesting to see his reaction when he discovered she was gone for the day, but unfortunately she could not be here to see it. Still, no doubt she would feel the aftermath when she got home that afternoon, and Lucinda could be relied upon to give her chapter and verse.

Two minutes later, a towel wrapped sarong-wise about her slim body, Holly ran down the steps to the beach. At this hour of the morning, the water was at its coolest, and it lapped about her deliciously as she dropped the towel and dived in. Swimming without the benefit of a bathing costume was something else she knew her father would abhor, and just occasionally she could see his point of view. But this bay was isolated; apart from herself and her servants there were no other inhabitants, and she and Samuel had swum together since they were children. Not that the Fletchers ever intruded on her privacy. In spite of the fact that they were like foster parents to her, they never took advantage of the fact. So far as she was concerned, it was an ideal arrangement, and if Morgan attempted to change it, he would find she was no longer the tongue-tied schoolgirl she used to be.

Fifteen minutes later, she squeezed the moisture out of her hair and, wrapping the towel around herself again, she returned to the house. 'Just toast and coffee, Luci,' she requested, putting her head round the kitchen door, and the housekeeper turned to look at her with undisguised disapproval.

'You been swimming like that?' she exclaimed, taking note of the towel, and Holly grimaced.

'I always do.'

'Not when we have guests you don't,' retorted

Lucinda, with the familiarity of their closeness. 'You know your Daddy's room overlooks the bay, just as yours does. You want that assistant of your father's to see you in the raw?'

'If he cares to look,' responded Holly irrepressibly, lifting one golden tanned shoulder. 'Did you hear what I said? Just toast and coffee for breakfast. I want to have my meal and be out of here before Mr Morgan Kane shows his face.'

Lucinda looked, if anything, even more reproachful. 'You ain't going over to Charlottesville today!' she protested fiercely. 'Holly, you know that man's come all this way to see you. You can't just walk out on him. Not on his first day!'

'Leave Mr Morgan Kane to me, will you, Luci?' Holly suggested lightly. 'Like I said, toast and coffee——'

'I heard what you said,' retorted Lucinda impatiently. She shook her head. 'I don't understand. Last night you seemed to be getting on with him real fine.'

'Last night?' Holly's lips tilted. 'Well, yes. But we didn't do much talking over supper. Mr Kane was too tired, and as soon as we'd finished, he went to bed.'

'I know that.' Lucinda sniffed. 'Oh, well. I suppose you know what you're doing. But your Daddy's not going to like this. He's not going to like it at all.'

Holly merely smiled and withdrew, but her smile disappeared as she ran up the stairs. Thank heavens Andrew Forsyth had never had a telephone connected to the house. Pulpit Island was reassuringly remote, and by the time Morgan guessed what she was doing, it wouldn't matter.

Although she normally took a shower after her swim, this morning she contented herself with simply washing her face and hands. The shower was noisy, and as it was next to Morgan's room, she couldn't afford the risk.

Besides, she didn't really have the time. In fifteen minutes she was downstairs again and seated at the kitchen table.

'Your hair's still wet,' said Lucinda, maintaining her disapproval, and Holly ran careless fingers over the hastily tied pony-tail.

'It will dry,' she said, spreading butter and peach jam on her toast. 'Did Micah check the radiator in the buggy? Yesterday it was running pretty hot.'

'He checked it,' said Lucinda laconically, apparently deciding she was wasting her time. 'And will you pick up the oil from Parrish's? As you're going in anyway, it will save Micah a journey.'

'I will.' Holly added cream to her coffee and took a considering sip. She didn't think she had forgotten anything. She had brought the exercise books downstairs the night before, and stowed them in her holdall in the hall. The text books she might need were already in there, along with the flask of iced tea Lucinda always made her.

'What time will you be wanting supper this evening?' asked the housekeeper now, folding her arms across her generous breasts. 'You will be in for supper, won't you? You ain't planning on spending the evening with the Brents?'

'Of course not.' Holly's eyes twinkled as she stuffed the remainder of the slice of toast into her mouth and sprang to her feet. 'Now—you look after Mr Kane for me, won't you?' she added mischievously. 'If he asks where I am, just tell him.'

'Oh, thanks.' Lucinda's tone was full of irony. 'That's good to know. I don't have to lie.'

'Would I ask you to do a thing like that?' asked Holly irrepressibly and, giving the black woman an affectionate hug, she sauntered out the door.

She met Micah in the cobbled yard at the back of the

house. As well as attending to the upkeep of the house, he also looked after the two cars, shared garden duties with Samuel, and cared for the animals. As well as the chickens and two goats, Holly had also managed to rescue three of the horses from her grandfather's stable. Left to run wild after her grandparent's death, the two mares and one stallion had not been easy to tame. But, with Micah's help, she had succeeded. Now, one of the mares had had a foal which Holly had called Hummingbird, and she could imagine what her father would say if he found out how she was spending the allowance he made her.

'You leaving?' Micah exclaimed in surprise when Holly shouldered her bag into the back of the little beach buggy, parked in the shade of a huge flame tree. 'Does Mr Kane know where you're going?'

'No, he doesn't,' said Holly flatly, unwilling to get involved in another argument. 'I'll see you later, hmm? After I've been to Parrish's.'

Micah's wide nostrils flared, but he made no comment, and Holly gave him a rueful smile. 'Trust me,' she said, reaching out to touch his sleeve, and the man shook his head somewhat resignedly before raising his hand in farewell.

The journey to Charlottesville was not quite as enjoyable as it usually was. Although she knew a sense of satisfaction at having outwitted Morgan Kane for today at least, Holly was aware of a troublesome sense of conscience. She couldn't afford to have a conscience, she told herself, as the buggy bounced its way along the forest track. People who wanted to succeed had to ignore the finer points of decency. Just because the Fletchers had some misguided notion that she should be polite to their visitor was no reason to be diverted from her purpose.

The road to Charlottesville took her through some of

the most beautiful scenery on the island. For a while after leaving the overgrown plantation, her route took her along a bluff overlooking the jagged rocks of Angel's Point. Once, when she was younger, she had asked her grandfather why the most dangerous part of the coastline should have been named Angel's Point, and he had laughed. 'Well, it's to be hoped the poor devils went to the angels,' he remarked, referring to the fishing boat which had floundered there only days before. 'You wouldn't want them going to the devil, now would you?'

From the point, the road turned inland again, skirting the sprawling mass of Pulpit rock before descending in a corkscrew to the little harbour town that nestled at its foot. Most of the residents of the island lived within a ten mile radius of Charlottesville, only the other planters like the Turners and the Brents having larger establishments further from town.

Holly was used to the road, which would have deterred the most enthusiastic of drivers, and reaching the comparatively gentle slopes above the harbour she drove more sedately to the Charlottesville Mission School. Here, she taught art and cookery three times a week, using the skills she had learned at the finishing school in Switzerland to teach boys as well as girls to appreciate the finer points of the culinary art. She doubted again whether her father would approve, but she didn't really care. Teaching had given her back her confidence, had made her aware of her own worth as a human being, and erased the blank uncertainty that had coloured her early years.

The Charlottesville Mission School was not really a mission school at all. Not any longer. It was supported by the local education department and the church authorities and, as island schools went, it was very good. The children were taught arts and crafts, as well as more academic subjects, and the percentage of pupils who went on to do further education on one of the larger islands was quite high. Holly had been teaching at the school for almost eighteen months now, ever since Stephen Brent had visited the house and seen her paintings.

The Brents and the Gantrys were the oldest families on the island. When Holly visited the island as a child, her grandmother used to take her to visit the Brents, and she and Stephen, and his younger sister, Constance, had all been friends. By the time Holly returned to the island however, Stephen's father was dead, too, and Stephen had married Verity Turner.

Even so, they were still friends, and it was Stephen who had suggested Holly should offer her talents to the education authorities. Although the Brent plantation was not in such a run-down state as the Gantry's, he himself spent four mornings a week at the school, teaching English and history, and their liking for one another had been cemented by their mutual interests.

Stephen's car was already parked on the dusty lot beside the schoolhouse when Holly drove the buggy in to join it. Although it was barely eight o'clock, school started early in the islands and, apart from a fifteen-minute break mid-morning, it continued, uninterrupted, until two o'clock.

As she got out of the buggy, Holly paused a moment to look at the view. She often did so thinking, as she did now, what an ideal location it was. Set above the harbour, with waving pandanus palms as a backcloth, and the sloping roofs of the little town sweeping down to the mast-dotted careenage below, it was an infinitely pleasant place to be, and she appreciated her good fortune. Determinedly putting all thoughts of her father and Morgan Kane to the back of her mind, she hoisted out her bag and crossed the sun-baked parking area, mounting the steps that led into the building with a slightly lighter heart.

She found Stephen in her classroom, propped against her desk, examining the sketches she had drawn for the play the children were hoping to produce at Easter. In his middle twenties, Stephen Brent was everything Morgan Kane was not, she thought reluctantly, despising herself for allowing that man's image to intrude yet again. Sturdily built, and about her own height, with curly brown hair and blue eyes, he was different in every way from the lean, dark-haired Englishman. Morgan Kane would top him, as he did her, by at least four inches, and whereas Stephen was broad and muscular, Morgan looked nothing like an athlete. Yet, for all that, he did have a toughness the West Indian lacked, a rapier-honed hardness that shortened the odds between them considerably. Holly suspected it was the life he had led—the constant changes from one time zone to another; the shortage of sleep; the hastily snatched meals; the ravages of junk food and alcohol, and too many late nights. But whatever it was, in any physical contest between them she would be loath not to choose Morgan as the victor; the simple result of any conflict between a sleckly fed tabby and an alley cat.

Ignoring the small voice inside her that probed her reasons for even contemplating such an eventuality, Holly walked firmly into the schoolroom and dropped her bag on the desk. 'Good morning,' she said, easing the straps off her aching shoulders, and Stephen looked up.

'Hi,' he said, surveying her somewhat windswept appearance with evident enjoyment. 'You look ready for anything. What happened? Didn't your visitor arrive?'

'Oh, he arrived all right.' Holly flopped down on to one of the children's chairs and pulled a face. 'How could you think otherwise? He is my father's creature, after all.'

Stephen looked sympathetic. 'And have you decided what you're going to do?' He frowned. 'You're not leaving, are you?'

Holly sighed. 'I don't know. It—depends.'

'On what?' Stephen put the sketches aside and straightened away from the desk. 'Surely your father can't make you do anything you don't want to. You're over eighteen, Holly.'

'I know.' She grimaced. 'But it's not that simple. I may be five thousand miles from England, but I'm still living in my father's house.'

'Mm.' Stephen grunted. 'That's what's so bloody unfair. I'm sure the Gantrys didn't intend Andrew Forsyth to get control of their property.'

'No.' Holly shrugged. 'Perhaps not. But they did give it to my mother before she died, never dreaming she would pre-decease them.'

'And your father inherited,' muttered Stephen grimly, shaking his head. 'It's barbaric!'

'Yes—well—' Holly made a dismissing gesture. 'That's all past history now. The house does belong to my father and there's nothing I can do about it. Not to mention the fact that my salary here is hardly enough to live on.'

'Money!' Stephen's jaw hardened. 'It all comes down to money, doesn't it? I bet that spineless pimp Forsyth has sent out to do his dirty work for him gets a damn sight more than you do!'

'I—wouldn't call Morgan Kane a spineless pimp,' murmured Holly reluctantly. 'Really. He's quite—nice.'

The word almost stuck in her throat, but it occurred to her that she might need Stephen's help to accomplish her purpose, and he would never agree to be a willing party to her subterfuge.

'*Nice!*' he echoed now, his lips twisting. 'Holly, how can you say the man is *nice*? He's a puppet! A yes-man! You said yourself he was your father's creature.'

'Well, yes, he is.' Holly licked her lips. 'But what else can he do, when all's said and done? My father is his employer, and—he does have a family to support.'

'You sound like you're defending him,' said Stephen coldly. 'Are you saying integrity has a price?'

Holly lifted a hand, palm outward, and rose abruptly to her feet. 'I'm only saying he has a job to do, and he's doing it. Be reasonable, Steve. I don't suppose you're proud of everything you've done in the cause of the Great God Mammon. I seem to remember the case of a family your father had evicted, just to appease Horace Turner.'

Stephen hunched his shoulders. 'That was different.'

'How was it different?'

'Turner was threatening to cut off our water supply, you know that. If he had, countless other families would have been affected.'

'So you consider the end justified the means?'

'In that case, yes.'

'Oh, Steve!' Holly gazed at him impatiently. 'Can't you see? Put Morgan's family in the place of your employees, and what have you got? An identical situation!'

'That was a long time ago, Holly.'

'I know.' Holly gave him a wry smile. 'Since when, you've married Verity Turner, and secured your irrigation rights.'

Stephen turned red. 'That wasn't why I married Verity, and you know it.'

'That's not what you said two weeks ago, when you drove me home from your house,' Holly reminded him flatly. Then, relenting, she ran her fingers lightly over the sun-bleached hairs on his arm. 'Oh—I'm sorry,' she said, realising she was being abominably cruel to someone who had always treated her with tenderness and affection. 'I don't mean to be bitchy, but you rubbed me up the wrong way. Just don't judge Morgan so harshly. He's only earning his salary.'

'You sound as if you're attracted to the man,' muttered Stephen grudgingly, his eyes moving possessively over the honey-gold skin exposed by her button-through poplin tunic. 'Since when did you call him by his first name? You always used to refer to him as *Mr* Kane.'

Holly had hardly been aware she had said Morgan, and now she found her own colour deepening. 'I mean—Morgan Kane, of course,' she said shortly, turning her attention to the contents of her holdall. 'Look, I really ought to be getting these things sorted out. The children are starting to arrive.'

Sure enough, a handful of boys and girls had already gathered in the playground, and Stephen regarded their presence with some impatience. 'All right,' he said. 'I realise we haven't got time to talk now, but in spite of everything, I want you to know I meant what I said.'

Holly stacked a pile of exercise books on the desk. 'Steve——'

'I mean it.' His hands clenched and she knew that, were their conversation not being monitored by a dozen pairs of dark eyes, he would have been more forceful. 'No matter how amusing it might seem to you, I do care about you, Holly. I wasn't just—making a pass, when I drove you home the other evening. All right, maybe my father did have something to do with my marrying Verity, but I did think I loved her then. It was only when you came back to the island—when I saw you again——'

'What's going on in here?'

To Holly's relief, Stephen's impassioned outburst was

stemmed by the arrival of a third party. Paul Bergerac
was another of the teachers at the school, an ex-pupil
himself, who had continued his education in the United
States and returned to the island a year ago to join the
staff. He came into the room now, his dark face alight
with curiosity, and Holly had the greatest difficulty in
finding a suitable excuse.

'Oh—Steve and I were just discussing the play,' she
tendered at last into the awkward silence that had
fallen. 'I—er—I've made some sketches of the costumes
I think we'll need, and we were wondering whether we'll
be able to find what we need in Charlottesv——'

'Bullshit!'

Stephen's angry protest interrupted the explanation
she was giving and, while Holly looked aghast at Paul's
grinning face, the other man charged out of the room.

'Oh, dear!' Paul was the first to recover himself, and
his teasing smile was reassuring. 'Methinks, the game's
afoot!' he misquoted, deliberately mixing his lines. 'Our
chief of men has been sent about with a flea in his ear!'

Holly shook her head. 'It's no joke, Paul. You don't
understand.'

'I understand that he's in love with you—or thinks he
is,' he retorted softly. 'We all are, you shameless
wench!' He chuckled. 'So, put us out of our misery:
which of us are you going to choose?'

'Oh, Paul!' A reluctant smile lifted the anxious
corners of her mouth. 'What would I do without you?'

'*Mon plaisir, mademoiselle*,' he responded gallantly,
effecting an exaggerated bow. 'Now, shall we invite the
pupils inside or shan't we? After all that drama, I don't
know if I can keep my mind on something as ordinary
as work!'

In spite of Holly's misgivings over the conversation
she had had with Stephen, the morning passed without
incident. Her painting lessons with the younger children

and more advanced charcoal sketching with the older ones took her up to break, and afterwards two cookery classes completed her schedule. She also helped Hannah Dessai, the sports mistress, with her games instruction, and made preparatory lists of the scenery they would need for the coming production. The school was like that. Although the staff had regular duties, they all took a part in the general running of the establishment. There were no lines of demarcation here. They all wanted to do the best they could for the eighty or so pupils.

To her relief, Stephen did not attempt to speak to her again privately before she left for home. At break, he was his usual friendly self, and she hoped she showed by her attitude that she appreciated his restraint. In all honesty, she had never taken Stephen seriously before. She had treated his overtures of affection with the inconsequence she had thought he expected, and she had been stunned to learn he had taken her remarks to heart. No doubt it was her fault, she sighed. She had initiated his declaration. But his hypocrisy had irritated her, and she had used the only means at her disposal to prick his pompous balloon.

The headmaster, Gerald Frost, caught her just as she was leaving. 'Oh, Miss Forsyth,' he said, loping across the car park towards her, his cassock flapping in the breeze. 'Could I have a word with you? It is rather important.'

'Of course,' said Holly, turning from loading her belongings into the buggy. She hoped it was nothing to do with Stephen. It would be terribly embarrassing if he had confided his feelings to someone else.

As well as being in charge of the small school, Reverend Frost was a minister of the Methodist church. A graduate of Trinity College, Oxford, he could have enjoyed a more academic career, but twenty years ago he had come to the island for a holiday and decided to stay. A shy man, he had never married, and his spare, angular figure was a familiar sight in Charlottesville. Paul always said—rather irreverently—that he wore his ecclesiastical robes like an actor wore his costume: because they provided a character he could hide behind.

'I'm so glad I caught you, Miss Forsyth,' he said now, panting a little as he came up to her. 'You're not in tomorrow, are you? Isn't it one of your free days?'

'That's right.' Holly nodded, still somewhat apprehensive. 'What can I do for you?'

'It's more in the nature of what I might be able to do for you,' murmured the headmaster ruefully. 'Stephen tells me you may be leaving.'

'Oh——' Holly's tongue circled her upper lip. 'Well, nothing's been decided yet.'

'No. So I understand.' Reverend Frost took a deep breath. 'But, if I were to speak to your father, explain what valuable work you're doing here, he might conceivably look more favourably on your desire to stay.'

Holly hesitated. 'What exactly did Stephen tell you, Reverend Frost?'

'Oh—only that your father is eager for you to return to London, and that you don't want to go.' He sighed. 'I can understand how he feels, of course. Your father, I mean. He must miss you terribly. I know I—we—would, if you were to leave.'

'Thank you.' Holly gave him a grateful smile. His suggestion was well meant, but she doubted it would carry much weight with Andrew Forsyth. Nevertheless, it was kind of him to make her feel wanted. It was not a sensation she had often experienced in her short life.

Looking into the minister's concerned face, she reflected on the irony that this man was probably only a couple of years older than Morgan Kane. Yet, she never thought of Reverend Frost as an equal. In all honesty, she seldom thought of him as a man at all. Not that he was at all effeminate, but simply because his sex was usually obscured by the character he had created for himself.

'Well, anyway,' he added now, 'if there is anything I can do, you have only to ask me.' A trace of colour entered his face, accentuating the freckles that arched across the bridge of his nose. 'I—we're all very fond of you, my dear. In a comparatively short space of time, you've become an integral part of our community.'

CHAPTER THREE

IT was almost four o'clock by the time Holly got back to the house. Calling for the oil at the chandlery had taken longer than she had anticipated, Mr Parrish insisting she couldn't leave without taking a glass of his home-made *maubi*. Although it was supposed to be non-alcoholic, the cocktail, derived from boiling tree bark, nutmeg and cinnamon, and adding it to a mixture of seagrape juice, ginger and cloves, was very potent, and Holly felt decidedly heady as she drove into the stable yard.

Still, it was not an unpleasant feeling, she reflected, lugging her heavy bag to the back door. In spite of her bravado, she had not been looking forward to facing Morgan Kane on her return. Now, however, she felt agreeably anaesthetised, and if her father's satellite was waiting for her, breathing fire, then she was suitably fortified against his wrath.

But to her surprise, and annoyance, Morgan was not there. 'He found that old sailing dinghy in the boat-house,' Lucinda informed her, not without a trace of smugness, lifting scones off the griddle on to a wire tray. 'Soon as he knew you wouldn't be back until this afternoon, he rigged up the sail and took himself off across the bay. I gave him a packed lunch, of course. So's he wouldn't get hungry.'

'How kind.' Holly's sarcasm was palpable. 'Who told him where the boat-house was?'

'No one did.' Lucinda shrugged. 'It's big enough to see, ain't it? And what with that hole rotting in the side, that padlock your Daddy put on it ain't much use.' She paused. 'Surely you don't mind, Holly. I can tell you, Mr Kane ain't the kind of man to sit around all day waiting for no woman.'

'Is that so?' Holly's lower lip jutted truculently. 'Well, I'm pleased to hear you've changed your mind about him. My father would be proud of you. It's exactly what he wanted.'

Lucinda straightened from the table, her dark eyes flashing indignantly. 'You've got no call to talk to me like that,' she exclaimed hotly. 'I'm not saying I like the man, and goodness knows, I don't want him whisking you off to London, you know that. But I did warn you it wasn't wise to antagonise him. He looked pretty tight-lipped when I told him where you'd gone.'

'Did he?' Holly's impatience with the housekeeper evaporated, and with a rueful gesture she put her arm around Lucinda's neck and hugged her. 'I'm sorry. I'm being totally unreasonable. But whenever my father takes a hand in my life, it's a disaster!'

'You can hardly blame your father for you jumping to the wrong conclusions,' pointed out Lucinda mildly, but she returned the girl's embrace and gently stroked her cheek. 'Now—I suggest you go and take a shower and tidy yourself up before Mr Kane gets back. Maybe if you take a bit of trouble with yourself, he'll overlook the fact that you've deliberately avoided him all day.'

Holly agreed, albeit for different motives and, after dumping her bag in her father's study, she went up to her room. She usually dawdled on the way, surveying her surroundings with loving eyes, but not today. For the first time, she was struck by the shabbiness of the paintwork, by the scars that marred the once-unblemished carvings, and by the worn patches in curtains which were probably older than she was. It was not an easy thing to admit, but she realised she was seeing the house with Morgan Kane's eyes. She despised herself for doing so, but she could no longer ignore the evidence before her. His intrusion had brought her back to the twentieth century as she used to know it; to thoughts of renovation and interior decoration; to a dissatisfaction with the house's neglect, and a latent desire to restore it to its former glory.

Not that she could ever have changed things on her own. The money her father sent her, and which she lavished so recklessly on the horses, would hardly have made an impression on the extensive repairs that were required. To restore even part of the house would have taken more than her yearly allowance, and she had long since learned not to ask her father for help. But that didn't help her now, when acceptance was giving way to frustration. Damn Morgan Kane, she thought. Damn him for coming here, and making her aware of the neglect. She had been contented enough until he made his entrance.

The room she was occupying had been her grandmother's room when Holly was a child. Like the room adjacent to it, on the other side of the bathroom, it had one of the best positions in the house, only getting the sun in the late afternoon, when much of the heat had gone out of it. It also enjoyed the most fantastic sunsets and, after her grandfather had died, Holly remembered her grandmother sitting on the balcony every evening, watching the sun go down.

The apartment had also been kept in a reasonably decent state of decoration. The dusty-pink damask wall hangings were still in good condition, and brightened by a handful of Holly's watercolours. Micah had framed the paintings for her, and they gave a more personal feel to the old-fashioned *armoire* and dressing-table, and the carved cheval mirror and dower chest which were so essentially Victorian in appearance.

Now, Holly unbuttoned her dress and, slipping it off her shoulders, she walked into the bathroom. She did feel hot and sticky, but instead of stepping into the shower, she bent and turned on the bath taps. The idea of soaking in a soapy tub was just too appealing, and if Morgan came back in the meantime, so what? He could hardly blame her, if he hadn't been around when she got home.

While the water ran into the circular bath, Holly cleaned her teeth and examined her profile in the mirror above the hand basin. What did Morgan Kane really think of her, she wondered. Did he still think of her as a kid, or had she convinced him she was a child no longer? Whatever his present opinion of her might be, she was committed to exploiting her appearance, and whether she succeeded or not, nothing was going to stop her from trying.

Stepping out of the scrap of silk that was all that still covered her she got into the bath, sinking down into the foaming bubbles. The water was scented, and the clouds of steam that rose about her perfumed the air with their own fragrance. The mirrors that lined the walls hazed, condensing the proportions of the room, and Holly relaxed completely. For a few moments she forgot all about her father—and Morgan Kane—and allowed her mind to drift without direction.

The unexpected invasion of her domain took her totally by surprise. One moment she was lying, idly watching the rainbow-coloured bubbles nudging the curve of her breast, and the next she was looking up into Morgan Kane's outraged face.

'For Christ's sake!' he muttered, backing off towards his bedroom. 'Couldn't you at least have locked the door?'

Although Holly was as shocked as he was by his unexpected intervention, the opportunity it afforded

was quickly absorbed. It was amazing, she mused. She
had thought her brain was dormant. But the minute she
looked up and met Morgan's dark grey eyes, the cells
sprang instantly into action.

'If I don't object, why should you?' she countered
softly, making sure her nipples were safely concealed
beneath the foam. 'Besides, there are no locks on these
doors. These rooms used to be used by my grandparents.'

Morgan's jaw compressed. 'You told me I was
occupying your father's room.'

'Well, you are,' said Holly carelessly. 'It's the master
bedroom. But he hardly ever uses it.'

'Even so——'

'Even so, nothing,' exclaimed Holly, lifting her arms
to release her hair from the elastic band she had secured that morning. She was beginning to enjoy
this, and there was a heady delight in knowing she
had the advantage. 'Don't be stuffy, Mr Kane,' she
teased. 'Surely you've seen a woman in the bath
before?'

Morgan's eyes, which had been so dark a few
moments earlier, now glittered angrily. He really was an
attractive animal, she thought unwillingly, forced, in
spite of herself, to an awareness of his undoubted
maleness. For all he must be forty-one or forty-two,
there was nothing soft about Morgan Kane. His body
was lean, and whipcord hard, with none of the
thickening around his waist that she had half expected.
Unlike the night before, when he had worn a suit more
fitted to an English boardroom than a tropical island,
he was wearing close-fitting white trousers and a short-
sleeved cotton-knit shirt, both of which bore traces of
seawater. His normally smoothly combed hair was
ruffled, and his skin gleamed with sweat. Although he
was not an excessively hairy man there were dark hairs

on his arms, curling about the leather strap of the watch that circled his wrist with loving insistence. And where his shirt fell open, it revealed a faint shading on his chest, a darker shadow that showed even through the cloth.

Holly was staring, but she couldn't help it, a curious *frission* that was half pleasure, half pain, stirring in the pit of her stomach. As her eyes dropped lower, over the muscles outlined beneath his taut trousers, she forgot everything but the illicit enjoyment she was gaining from just looking at him, and the muffled oath he uttered before slamming out of the room took several minutes to penetrate.

When it did, Holly found to her annoyance that her hands were trembling. As she reached for the soap, it slid elusively away between her fingers, and she had to grope for it in the water, dislodging a load of bubbles in the process. Damn, she thought irritably, rescuing the soap at last; it was not part of her plan that she should become attracted to him. The hopeless passion she had nurtured in her school-days was dead and buried, and she must not allow herself to be diverted by his physical appearance. He was attractive, it was true, but she had known attractive men before, and it wasn't as if she was starved of male admiration. The idea was that he should be attracted to her, and to that end she had made a promising beginning. There had been a definite awareness in that initial look he gave her, and she had certainly proved to him that she was not a child.

Deciding it would be safer to meet him again downstairs, Holly wrapped a towel about herself and retired to her own bedroom after her bath. The temptation to reverse their positions was appealing, particularly when she heard Morgan in the bathroom, but she resisted it. She told herself it was because she didn't want to rush things, but that wasn't entirely true.

In all honesty, she needed time to compose herself, and she had no intention of ruining her plans trying to prove her indifference.

It was too early for supper and, as she wanted to give Morgan the opportunity to think about what had happened, Holly spent some time drying her hair and applying a pearlised polish to her nails. She also took some trouble over her make-up, using a bronze lustre over the arch of her brows and a darker shadow on her lids. With her pale hair the contrast was very successful. It toned well with the full-sleeved shirt and tie-waisted trousers she was wearing, both made of a coffee-brown raw silk fabric.

With low-heeled strappy sandals to complete her outfit, Holly eventually went downstairs at about a quarter to seven. Moving with sinuous grace across the hall, she was aware of the unmistakable quickening of her blood at the thought of seeing Morgan again, and she chided herself impatiently for allowing emotion to colour her judgment.

Although she thought he might be on the verandah, he wasn't, and she turned instead to the small, family dining room where they had eaten the night before. But he wasn't there either, and she was just beginning to feel anxious when he appeared in the doorway of her father's study.

Apart from the living room and the dining room, Andrew Forsyth's study was the only other room used with any frequency on the ground floor, but she resented his assumption that he could use it as his right.

'Looking for me?' he enquired, his voice low and lacking in expression, and she had to bite back the angry retort that sprang to her lips.

'I—wondered where you were,' she amended smoothly, pushing her hands into the waistline pockets of her trousers. 'You soon find your way around, Mr Kane.'

'I had plenty of time,' he responded, propping his shoulder against the jamb, 'You don't mind me using your father's study, I assume. He has given me power of attorney to act on his behalf.'

'Why should I?' Holly had succeeded in controlling her temper, and when she approached him, he fell back to allow her to enter the room. She noticed the tray of drinks on the cabinet and permitted a tight smile. 'I see Lucinda has been looking after you. I hope you made yourself at home.'

'I have.' Morgan straightened away from the door, and now she saw the half-empty glass in his hand. 'Can I fix you a drink? We seem to have everything.'

Holly hesitated a moment, stung by his assumption of command, and then she relaxed. 'Why not?' she acknowledged, walking to the french doors that opened on to the verandah and guessing he had seen her looking for him. She turned back and seated herself in a buttoned leather armchair. 'I'll have some wine, please.'

'White, of course,' said Morgan, examining the bottles on the tray. 'My ex-wife drinks white wine. It's become quite fashionable to do so.'

Holly tilted her head. 'And is your ex-wife fashionable, Mr Kane?' she enquired, guessing he had brought her up deliberately, to put her in her place. She was gratified by the distinct hollowing of his cheekbones as he sucked in his breath at her implied insolence. But his expression was unrewarding as he handed her her glass.

'I think so,' he replied evenly, meeting her gaze with narrowed eyes. 'Now—can we cut the small talk and get down to business? I didn't come here to discuss my personal affairs.'

'You brought her up,' Holly reminded him softly, allowing her tongue to touch the rim of the glass, and Morgan sighed. Expelling his breath heavily, he walked to the desk and eased his weight on to one corner. Then, with a gesture of resignation, he swallowed the remaining liquid in his glass.

Tonight, he had reverted to the lounge suit he had worn the previous evening, but without the benefit of the waistcoat. Lucinda must have pressed it for him, for there were no signs of creasing in the jacket that fitted his shoulders like a glove. A grey silk shirt and matching tie completed his apparel, and Holly was not unaware of how well his clothing suited him. But then, she reflected somewhat dourly, he looked good in anything. She rather thought he would look equally good without his clothes, and as her cheeks deepened with becoming colour, she was glad he was not observing her so closely.

'Where did you go today?' he asked at length, looking across at her, and Holly lifted her shoulders.

'I thought Lucinda told you.'

'I'm asking you.'

'Oh——' She shrugged and got up from her seat again. 'I went to Charlottesville. It was a standing arrangement. I couldn't get out of it.'

'What kind of standing arrangement?'

'Don't you know?'

Morgan sustained her enquiring gaze without flinching. 'You tell me.'

Holly sighed. 'Very well. I teach at the mission school there.'

Morgan inclined his head. 'Very commendable.'

'Don't patronise me!'

The words were out before she could prevent them, and she thought she saw the glimmer of a smile touch his lean mouth. Damn him! she thought again, resenting his apparent mastery of their conversation. She had had the advantage. Where had it gone?

'I mean it,' he said now, putting his empty glass aside

and linking his hands loosely between the parting of his legs. 'I didn't realise you had a job.'

'It's not a job,' said Holly flatly, taking a sip of her wine. 'At least—well, I enjoy it. I like working with children. They're so—uncomplicated.'

'And is your life so complicated?' enquired Morgan drily, looking up at her. 'I wouldn't have thought so.'

'But you don't know what my life is like,' retorted Holly quickly, and then, drawing back from a more vituperative retaliation, she added, 'Do you?'

Morgan half smiled. 'I guess not.'

'You only know what my father tells you, right?'

'Right.' He was conciliatory. 'But I do read his correspondence and make my own interpretation of the facts.'

'I rarely write to my father,' said Holly at once, and he tipped his head to one side.

'I know that.'

'So you know very little about me.'

'I pay your allowance—or rather, I arrange for it to be paid,' he amended mildly, and she stared at him with troubled eyes.

'You—pay my bills?'

'Would you rather someone else did?'

Holly expelled her breath on a gasp. 'I thought—my father——'

'That's what he employs an accountant for,' remarked Morgan without emotion. 'Relax. It's all quite normal, I assure you.'

Holly's lips compressed. 'Of course. You would say that. I suppose you pay your own salary, too.'

'I suppose I do,' agreed Morgan evenly. 'But I think that's enough about financial matters for the present. I want to talk to you about something else.'

Holly set down her glass on the desk and gave him a guarded look. 'I know you do,' she said, forcing herself to remain there, only an arm's length away from him. 'I didn't think you'd flown all this way just to enjoy my company. You wouldn't do that, would you, Mr Kane? That's not why my father sent you.'

'Holly——'

'If you can call me Holly, can I call you Morgan?' she interrupted him abruptly, turning fully to face him. 'I mean—it's not as if we're not old friends, is it? I felt I knew you even before we actually met face to face.'

His lips thinned. 'If it pleases you.'

'It does.' Holly felt the excitement of feeling she was gaining the ascendancy again. 'Morgan.' She smiled. 'That's a well-known name in these islands—though not usually a well-loved one, I have to say.'

Morgan sighed. 'Why are you doing this?'

'Doing this? Doing what?' Holly regarded him innocently and he got slowly to his feet.

'This,' he said succinctly, making no attempt to move away from her, and her pulses fluttered at his disruptive nearness. 'You shouldn't start things you can't finish, Holly. You haven't got the experience.'

'And you have,' she murmured breathily, doing her best to appear casual, and he gave her a weary look.

'Let's say I understand the situation better than you do,' he conceded flatly. 'Now—do you want to start again?'

She was forced to look up to meet his eyes, and her senses stirred at the searching appraisal of his gaze. She had never been this close to him before, and it was quite unnerving. It wasn't just that he was a disturbing influence; she was also aware of who he was, and what he could do to her if he related this conversation to her father. And he was also so much older than she was, when all the men she had ever associated with had been contemporaries of hers.

'You're a very—attractive man,' she managed to say

at last, her hands pushed once more into her pockets to disguise their trembling. 'I've always thought so.'

'Really?' Morgan did not sound convinced. 'But I am also twenty years older than you are, and that much wiser.'

Holly held up her head. 'So?'

'So I don't play games with little girls,' he said quietly, exploding all her hopes. 'And what's more, I don't believe you mean a word of what you're saying. I think this is just another ploy to avoid discussing the reason that brought me here, but if you're desperate for sexual activity, I suggest you find someone of your own age to practise with.'

Holly's temper flared, but before she could think of a suitable retort, Lucinda put her head around the door. An expression of astonishment crossed her face as her sharp eyes took in their close proximity, and Morgan made a sound of impatience before putting Holly firmly aside.

'Yes?'

'Er—meal's on the table,' said the housekeeper, with her usual lack of formality. 'And I chilled another bottle of that hock, Mr Kane, just like you told me.'

'Thank you.' Morgan's acknowledgment would have oiled the buggy for a month, thought Holly frustratedly. 'We're coming now,' he added, equally smoothly. 'Holly, will you lead the way?'

Lucinda had taken trouble with the table, putting out the best linen and polishing the cutlery to a high shine. She had even made a centrepiece of scarlet hibiscus and creamy white oleander, threading the two together with feathery strands of fern. The first course of pink-lined shells of papaw, filled with a cocktail of pineapple, celery and prawns, was already waiting on conch-shaped dishes, but Holly hardly noticed. All she could think was how stupid she had been to underestimate her adversary. She should have known that someone her father trusted so implicitly was unlikely to be deceived by her amateurish overtures. If she wanted Morgan Kane to take her seriously, she had to be more subtle. But how could she be subtle when she had so little time?

She only picked at the papaw cocktail, and left most of the chopped chicken and beef that followed it. She noticed once that Morgan did not appear to be hungry either, but he seemed to enjoy the wine and so did she. It was something to do with her hands in the long intervals between courses, a fragile barrier perhaps, but a barrier nevertheless, between her uncertainty and Morgan's impatience.

'Are you going to speak to me?' he remarked at last, after Lucinda had cleared their plates with an offended air. 'You haven't even asked me how your father is keeping. Don't you care?'

Holly shrugged. 'Does he care about me?'

'That's a stupid question.'

'Is it?' Her artificially darkened brows arched. 'Since when have I figured highly in his scheme of things?'

'Your father's a busy man.'

'Oh, yes, I know.' Holly grimaced. 'He's busy making money, and getting married, and trying to produce an heir! Oh, yes,' she added bitterly, twisting her wine glass between her fingers, 'I know all about his efforts in that direction. His last wife—what was her name? Cherry? Yes, that's right. Cherry put me squarely in the picture. What a pity it didn't work out. He couldn't impregnate her, either.'

'That will do.' Morgan's mouth snapped shut. 'I don't find this kind of conversation amusing.'

'Nor do I.' Holly met his eyes defensively. 'But when a girl not much older than you are starts telling you she's going to be the one to put you out of the picture, you can't help feeling a little—*pleased*, when it doesn't happen.'

Morgan sighed. 'Well, that was not what I wanted to talk to you about.'

'I know.' Holly's tongue appeared momentarily. 'But you didn't have any problems in producing an heir, did you, Morgan? You produced two of them.'

Morgan regarded her resignedly. 'You won't give it up, will you?'

'Do you want me to?' Holly couldn't resist the taunt.

'You know I do.'

'All right. Let's talk about something else. Would you like me to give you a résumé of my activities since I came to the island? Just to put my father in the picture?'

'You can tell him yourself,' said Morgan flatly. 'You did get his telegram, didn't you?'

'I think this is where I came in,' said Holly, pushing back her chair and getting to her feet. 'Do you mind if I skip coffee? I suddenly have the most annoying heada——'

His fingers caught her wrist as she would have left the table, curving strong and brown about her skin. They crushed the sensitive pulse that beat with increasing irregularity against his palm, and dug into the flesh that protected the network of veins.

'I mind,' he said, looking up at her with dark impatient eyes. 'Holly, this isn't going to work.' He expelled his breath on a sigh, and its wine-tainted warmth swept over her. 'I've been here more than twenty-four hours and we've hardly touched on the reasons why I'm here.'

'I'm tired,' said Holly, making a perfunctory effort to free herself. 'And—and I do have a headache. It was very hot in Charlottesville this afternoon and David Parrish's *maubi* didn't help.'

Morgan frowned. *'Maubi?'*

'It's a drink they make here on the island. It's not supposed to be alcoholic, but I think it is.'

Morgan's nostrils flared. 'And who is David Parrish? A boyfriend?'

'A boyfriend?' Holly couldn't prevent a gurgle of amusement from escaping her. The idea that David Parrish, who must be sixty if he was a day and portly with it, might be considered a boyfriend, was just too ridiculous to ignore.

'Who is he then?' enquired Morgan, his tightening grip warning her that he did not find her humour at all amusing. Holly winced.

'Wouldn't you like to know,' she retorted, gazing down at her steadily whitening hand. 'You know, if you don't let go of me soon, my fingers may just drop off.'

Morgan's eyes dropped to his possession of her wrist, and, noticing the reddening above his fingers and the bloodless state of her hand below, he relaxed his grip. But he did not let her go, and as the life-giving fluid flowed back into her veins, she had to suffer the agony without being able to ease it.

'Tell me about David Parrish,' he said, his thumb moving almost absently over the back of her hand. 'I gather he's not the reason you don't want to leave the island. Who is he? One of the other teachers at the school?'

'He keeps a store in Charlottesville,' muttered Holly unwillingly, half afraid that, if she refused to answer him, he would tighten his grip again. Already, she was sure there would be a bruise on her arm tomorrow, and she had no desire for another demonstration of his undoubted strength. 'He's old and fat and—married.'

Morgan seemed to become aware that he was stroking the back of her hand, and released her. 'Old and fat, and married,' he echoed drily. 'A damning accusation! Do I detect a more personal allusion?'

Holly hesitated, rubbing her wrist. Now that she was free, the desire to leave him was not as strong. 'You know that's not what I meant,' she mumbled sulkily.

'Do I?' Morgan lay back in his chair, regarding her with unexpected indulgence. 'I expect I am overweight, too.' He rubbed his midriff reflectively. 'Middle-aged men usually are.'

Holly sighed. 'You don't look middle-aged and you know it.'

'But I *am* middle-aged,' retorted Morgan, swinging forward in his seat again and meeting her startled gaze. 'I'm forty-one, Holly; almost forty-two! That should mean something to you. I'm old enough to be your father, more than old enough! And believe me, you wouldn't like it if I started taking you seriously.'

Holly sniffed. 'You're a lot like my father, too, aren't you, Mr Kane?' she responded, a suspiciously husky note in her voice. 'He doesn't have any emotions either. How do you regard feelings, I wonder? As an unnecessary weakness?'

'Oh, *God*!' With a groan of frustration, Morgan got up from his chair and confronted her. 'You couldn't be more wrong! I have feelings; of course, I have. If I didn't, I wouldn't be letting you put me on like this.'

'Put you on?' she echoed, and he nodded.

'Okay,' he said wearily. 'We won't discuss your father's wishes tonight. You'd better go to bed. If you have got a headache, I don't want to be held responsible for making it worse.'

Holly quivered, wishing she could take back her reckless words. She didn't really have a headache; and if Morgan was prepared to wait until tomorrow before bringing up her father's invitation, she would just as soon stay here and talk to him.

But she couldn't say that, not and run the risk of being called a liar. Instead, she had to take her dismissal gladly, and be grateful for the time to consider what his tantalising words had meant.

CHAPTER FOUR

MORGAN kicked off his training shoes and walked slowly down to the water's edge. It was early—very early—and the air was as sweet and crisp as a good wine. On the horizon, the clouds were turning through dark blue and amber to palest yellow, the line of the ocean reflecting the colour of the sky.

Closer at hand, dozens of tiny sand crabs scuttled out of his path and a group of sea-birds squabbled over the remains of a turtle washed up by the tide. Scavengers, he thought; every continent had them. And not all of them animal, he reflected, recalling the scramble for shares on the floor of the Stock Exchange.

Sighing, he threaded long fingers into his hair and pushed it back from his temple. He would not think about Andrew's orders right now. It was too early in the day to start wondering how he was going to make Holly agree to the situation. He half wished today was yesterday and he could escape again for a few relaxing hours.

He should have brought his swimming gear, he mused regretfully, looking down at the stained white trousers which had been his only concession to his destination. But then, he had not expected to be here longer than a couple of days and, because he had anticipated a hostile welcome, he had brought a minimum of clothing.

It hadn't been so bad the previous day. He had sailed the dinghy clear across the bay before stripping off his clothes and diving over the side. The water had felt so good against his hot skin, and it had been his first experience of swimming in the raw.

He glanced consideringly at his watch. It was only half past six. He doubted Holly would appear for hours yet, knowing that today he was not going to be put off with any more excuses. The steepness of the cliff protected all but a narrow strip of beach from prying eyes. If he undressed in the shadow of the overhang, who was likely to see him?

Before he could succumb to second thoughts, Morgan pulled the knitted cotton shirt over his head and dropped it on to the sand. Then he unzipped his trousers and stepped out of them, peeling off his briefs and tossing them on to the small pile, too. He ran into the water, plunging head first into the waves. He swam strongly away from the beach, not stopping until he felt sufficiently safe from exposure. There was always the chance that one of the servants might see him, and he had no desire for Holly to learn he had been caught in embarrassing circumstances.

He turned on to his back, feeling the strengthening heat of the sun warming his pleasantly chilled body. It was delightful to allow himself to drift with the tide, and he gave no thought to any possible dangers until there was a splashing in the water close beside him.

Immediately, the realisation that there could be sharks in these southerly waters brought him jack-knifing to a position where he could tread water. Jerking his head round, he ascertained that there were no suspicious fins lurking anywhere about him, and he was just about to abandon his search when a sleek wet head surfaced beside him.

'Holly!' he exclaimed blankly, as her arm came up to sweep her hair out of her eyes, and she laughed.

'Did I frighten you?' she taunted, using lazily circular motions of her hands to keep her afloat. 'I'm sorry. I thought you were Samuel.'

Morgan recovered himself with an effort, unavoidably

aware that she was as naked as he was. The curve of her bosom gleamed dully beneath the blue-green water, that part of her body so much paler than the honey-gold tan of her limbs.

'Do you usually swim with Samuel?' he enquired tersely, conscious of a totally unreasonable sense of outrage, and she shrugged.

'Sometimes. But, he doesn't swim in the nude—in case you're interested.'

Morgan tensed. 'Why should I be interested?'

'I don't know.' Her lips parted provocatively. 'But you are, aren't you?'

Morgan forced himself to sustain her challenging gaze. 'If I'm concerned, it's because of what your father would think if he knew,' he retorted shortly. 'You want me to treat you as an adult, yet you persist in behaving like a child.'

'How?' Holly's eyes widened indignantly. 'By swimming in the way we were intended?' She paused a moment, and then added insinuatively, 'As you're doing.'

The darker circles that defined the peaks of her breasts were outlined distinctly as she turned and started to swim easily towards the shore. And to Morgan's intense frustration, he felt his own involuntary reaction. *'For Christ's sake,'* he berated himself savagely, plunging down into the water, so that the chillier depths cooled his heated blood. Andrew would have a fit if he knew what he was thinking. The girl was deliberately trying to provoke him, he knew that. And he had played directly into her hands by giving in to a wholly uncharacteristic impulse.

Nevertheless, he could not prevent his eyes from turning in her direction when she reached the beach. He was simply checking to make sure she was not intercepted, he told himself impatiently, as she stepped proudly out of the water, but it wasn't altogether true. Even from a distance, her spine, and the downy curve of her buttocks were infinitely disturbing, and he would not have been human if he had not found them good to look upon.

She had apparently left a towel on the sand, and now she lifted the buttercup yellow folds and wrapped them about her. Then she turned and looked at him, revealing that she had been aware of his appraisal all along.

'Don't you have a towel?' she called, having observed his pile of clothes, and Morgan wondered if she intended confiscating his belongings, just to get her own back.

'No,' he shouted in return, wishing he had reached the beach first. 'It's all right. I don't need one.'

'Don't be silly,' she retorted. 'You'll wet all your clothes. I tell you what—I'll put your clothes on, and leave the towel for you.'

'No——'

But Morgan's immediate denial was ignored. He watched with blank impotence as Holly shed the enveloping towelling and stepped into his trousers, knotting the belt about her waist before reaching for his shirt.

'What do you think?' she called, doing a pirouette for his benefit, and Morgan's teeth clenched.

'I'll see you later,' he muttered, not loud enough for her to hear, and with a gurgle of enjoyment, Holly sauntered away towards the steps.

Morgan did not see Holly on his way up to his room. To his relief, he did not see anyone, and he breathed a sigh of satisfaction when the door had closed behind him. Even so, he did not shed the towel until he had ascertained that the bathroom was empty. Then, he stepped swiftly into the shower cubicle, securing the catch before turning on the jets.

It was good to rinse all the salt from his body, and he stood for some time in the spray, allowing the needle-sharp power of the water to massage his skin. It had a soothing effect, and by the time he emerged to wrap a clean towel around his hips, he felt less aggressive about Holly's intervention.

She had not returned his clothes, however, and he was just thinking he would have to wear the trousers of his suit when he saw the sawn-off denims on the bed. There was a note beside them which read:

> These are Samuel's, but he says you can borrow them. At least, until you can buy a pair in town. I would have lent you some clothes of my father's, but I'm sure you wouldn't have liked it when they slipped down off your hips.

Morgan's mouth drew down sardonically at her deliberate reference to her father's girth. Andrew was overweight, there was no denying it, but it wasn't really kind to imply that her father's waist was wider than his hips. And how could he wear Samuel's trousers? he asked himself impatiently. Size-wise, there might not be much to choose between them. But he was here on business, and knee-length denims were not the attire of someone who wanted to be taken seriously. What the hell had she done with his own trousers? Why couldn't she simply have returned his clothes to him? It wasn't as if she needed to wear them. Judging by her appearance last night, she had plenty of clothes to choose from.

With a feeling of irritation, he started towards the wardrobe to get his suit, and then took a second look at the denims. The idea of wearing someone else's trousers was not appealing, but they were newly laundered, and he was not attracted by his alternative. With a sigh, he dropped the towel and thrust his legs into the jeans, hauling them up over his narrow hips. Dear God, he thought, as they moulded the powerful muscles of his thighs. He couldn't wear these, they were almost indecent.

He sighed, surveying his appearance in the long mirror of the wardrobe. The trousers barely covered his hips, exposing his navel and the start of the hair on his stomach. For the rest, he was relieved to see no obvious thickening of the flesh below his rib-cage, even though that morning's swim had left the muscles of his midriff protesting. And because of his dark colouring, he did not look too anaemic, he thought, his frequent trips to hotter climes supplementing his natural skin tones.

Even so, the idea of appearing in public in such outrageous gear was a powerful deterrent. He wouldn't put it past Holly to have arranged the whole thing, he thought irritably, which was a little unfair considering he had set the scene himself. Nevertheless, it was two days since he had left London, and he had to get down to the purpose of his visit. Going about in the kind of clothes more suited to a Caribbean *holiday* might look more casual, but it was not the way Andrew would expect him to conduct his business.

A tap at the door stilled his hands before they could unfasten the metal button that secured the waistband. Guessing it was Holly, come to survey her handiwork, Morgan was not amused, and his harsh, 'What do you want?' contained none of his usual amicability.

'You want I should bring your breakfast upstairs, Mr Kane?' came Lucinda's aggrieved tones, and Morgan uttered an oath. Striding to the door, he jerked it open, and not until the housekeeper's lips formed a round 'O' did he realise he had forgotten what he was wearing.

'Lucinda, I——'

'Well, don't you look nice?' exclaimed the black woman, interrupting him. 'Them's Samuel's trousers, ain't they? Holly said as how they would fit you, and they do.'

'Hardly,' said Morgan drily, aware of the stain of embarrassment in his cheeks. 'I—er—I think they're too tight, don't you? But it was kind of your son to——'

'They're not too tight,' Lucinda protested. 'Denim's like that. Straight after washing, it needs a little time to wear in.' She paused. ''Course, if you don't think they're good enough . . .'

Morgan's smile was forced, but inside he was seething with resentment. Holly might not have arranged this situation, but she was sure as hell taking advantage of it, he thought. Why else would Lucinda come knocking on his door at half past seven in the morning, when the previous day he hadn't taken breakfast until a couple of hours later?

'Well,' he said narrowly, 'if you think they look all right.'

'I do.' Lucinda nodded her head and gave him an old-fashioned look. 'So long as you've got it, flaunt it, isn't that what they say?' she chuckled. 'I'll have the pancakes on the table in fifteen minutes.'

Morgan closed the door behind her with a controlled click. If he could have got his hands on Holly at that moment, he was sure he would have choked her. Now he was committed to wearing the bloody things! he thought angrily. Either that, or lose Lucinda as a possible ally.

It didn't altogether surprise him to find Holly waiting for him at the table. She had evidently taken a quick shower, too, for her oval face was gleaming with good health, and her hair had none of the stickiness associated with salt water. She had shed his shirt and trousers in favour of a white, sleeveless vest and thigh-hugging Bermudas, and she looked up at him with some amusement as he came into the room.

'They suit you,' she said, surveying his appearance with some satisfaction. 'Leastways, the cut-offs do. I'm not so happy with your choice of top.'

'Your opinion isn't that important to me,' retorted Morgan shortly, taking his seat at the table. 'You may have noticed, I didn't come prepared for a long visit. And you appear to have filched my only informal attire.'

'Lucinda's washing them,' said Holly carelessly, propping her chin on one hand and regarding him thoughtfully. 'Couldn't you do without a shirt? Lots of people do.'

'All male, I hope,' remarked Morgan drily, unable to deny the wry insertion, and Holly smiled.

'Usually,' she acknowledged, 'although there are beaches on the islands where people do go topless. It's not exactly encouraged, but what can the authorities do?'

Morgan assumed an interest in the napkin he was spreading on his lap to avoid a response, and Lucinda's appearance with a huge plate of pancakes negated the necessity. The dish of fresh berries she placed on the table, together with a jug of maple syrup and another of cream, demanded an acknowledgment, and Holly licked her lips in anticipation. 'Is it me or Mr Kane you're hoping to fatten up?' she exclaimed, as the housekeeper set a pot of coffee at her elbow. 'You know I adore pancakes, but they really are too rich.'

'Seems like either one of you could stand a little more flesh on your bones,' retorted Lucinda, unrepentant. 'If there's anything else you need, Mr Kane, you just holler.'

Morgan smiled, but he couldn't help wondering what Andrew would say if he could see him now. No doubt the older man was already growing impatient because Morgan hadn't been in touch with him. He wondered if he ought not to find the post office and telex him what had happened so far.

'One or two?' Holly was asking now, and Morgan dragged his thoughts back to the present.

'Just one to begin with,' he accepted, eyeing the thick wedges with some misgivings. It was just as well he had done some exercise that morning. At this rate, he'd gain weight whether he liked it or not.

Holly served the pancakes, adding maple syrup to his after only a momentary hesitation. 'The traditional way,' she said, passing the plate to him. 'They don't make pancakes like this in England.'

Morgan could believe it. The pancakes his mother used to make when he was a child had been much more modest, and Alison had only ever produced a French-style crêpe, which was definitely crisper. But Lucinda's offerings were delicious, and he found himself accepting a second, when he ought not to have eaten the first.

'Good, mm?' Holly said, and he nodded, realising as he did so that he would not be getting in touch with Andrew today. His conscience simply would not allow him to loose her father's anger upon her, not until he had put the situation to her. He would send word to Andrew tomorrow, when he knew for certain when they would be back.

He was finishing his third cup of coffee, and feeling unpleasantly bloated, when Holly asked, 'Do you ride?'

'Ride?' Morgan put his cup aside. 'I assume you mean horses.'

'Well, we don't have anything else here,' responded Holly ruefully. 'Do you?'

Morgan shrugged. 'Why?'

'Answer me, and I'll tell you.'

'Well——' Morgan grimaced. 'I went pony-trekking once, about twenty years ago. But—it wasn't an unqualified success.'

'Why not? Didn't you like it?'

Morgan hesitated, doubtful whether he ought to tell her the truth. 'The—er—the friend I went with didn't like it,' he admitted. 'I spent most of my time fishing——' he baulked, 'fishing *him* out of ditches.'

'Him?' Holly regarded him through half-closed lids, and Morgan sighed.

'All right, *her*, then. Whatever, it wasn't a holiday I remember with any affection.'

Holly drew her lower lip between her teeth. 'Was that your wife?' she asked carefully, and Morgan bent his head.

'No,' he said at last, looking up at her again. 'She was just a girlfriend. Someone I used to work with.'

'At Forsyth's?'

'Yes.' Morgan was growing a little impatient now. 'That really isn't at issue, is it? You asked if I rode, and I've told you. I don't.'

'Riding is riding. Once you've learned to sit a horse, you don't forget.'

'I doubt if the purists would agree with you,' remarked Morgan evenly. 'However, now that we've established the facts, why did you ask?'

'Come and see my horses,' said Holly, getting to her feet.

'*Your* horses?' Morgan frowned. 'I understood your father let the horses go, when your grandparents died.'

Holly pressed her lips together. 'He did. But I rescued them. Come and see them, please. One of the mares has had a foal.'

Morgan came to his feet with some reluctance. 'But how have you managed to keep a couple of horses?' he protested, and she grinned.

'Not two horses, four,' she corrected him gleefully. 'Come on. I'll show you where we keep them. Micah and Samuel help me to look after them, you see.'

The stables were across a cobbled yard. The yard itself was sheltered by a wall, with fruit trees espaliered to its crumbling brickwork. Chickens pecked about the roots of a huge live oak, and there was a moist, earthy scent to the air.

The two mares, and the stallion which Holly told him was called Trader, each occupied separate stalls opening on to a central aisle. Adjoining the stables was a corralled yard where the animals could exercise, but Holly explained that she and Samuel took them out at least twice a week.

'It should be more, I know,' she said, opening the gate into the larger stall where the mare, Bonnie, and her foal were housed. 'Mm, who's a handsome boy, then?' she added, as the young colt nudged her pocket. 'Here you are.' She produced a sugar lump. 'And for you, Bonnie.' She stroked the mare's nose and glanced at Morgan over her shoulder. 'Aren't they beautiful? Could you just abandon them?'

Morgan came to make friends with the mare, taking the lump of sugar Holly offered, and holding it on his palm. 'I gather your father doesn't know about this,' he remarked, feeling as if he was letting her down, and Holly's face sobered.

'No,' she said. 'No, he doesn't. Or rather he *didn't*. I assume you mean you're going to tell him.'

'I didn't say that,' murmured Morgan mildly, but all the same he knew he should. 'What does it cost to feed a horse of this size these days? And where are you getting the money to do it?'

Holly led the way out of the stall and closed the gate. 'I'm not stealing it, if that's what you mean,' she retorted, a little huffily. 'What I do with my allowance is my affair, surely.'

Morgan inclined his head. 'Your father wondered why you asked for a raise six months ago. I believe he thought you must be buying a lot of clothes.'

'I don't need many clothes here,' she replied, moving to the adjoining cubicle. 'And I do get a small sum for teaching at the school.'

Morgan absorbed this as she made a fuss of the mare next door. 'This is Athena,' she said, producing more sugar from her pocket. 'She's the most gentle of beasts.' She paused, and then added softly 'Do you think you could ride her?'

'Me?' Morgan gasped. 'Holly, if that's what this is leading up——'

'Why not?' She gazed at him entreatingly, her silky cheek resting against the mare's well-groomed head. 'Just for an hour,' she begged. 'I could show you the plantation. There's not much of it left now, but you might find it interesting.'

'Holly——'

'Please, Morgan!'

The indigo eyes were warm and appealing and, although it was against his better judgment, Morgan found himself giving in. 'All right,' he said, glancing at his watch.'But just for an hour. And then you agree we talk about why your father sent me.'

Holly hunched her shoulders. 'All right,' she said offhandedly. 'I'll tell Lucinda where we're going. Here's Samuel. He'll saddle the horses for us. Trader for me, please, Sam. And Athena for Mr Kane.'

The boy—Morgan guessed he was probably still in his teens—regarded the newcomer without liking. Morgan suspected Samuel resented the fact that he was going riding with his mistress, instead of himself, and he was tempted to suggest the boy took his place. Only the suspicion that Holly might not keep to their agreement if he let them go alone prevented him from offering, and he met the boy's sullen gaze with a conciliatory smile.

'Er—thanks for lending me your jeans,' Morgan ventured awkwardly, as Samuel brought the bay stallion out of its stall, and the boy shrugged.

''S'all right,' he responded, fastening the girth with an expert hand. 'Miss Holly said I should. She said you didn't realise you'd be staying so long.'

'No. That's right.' Morgan wondered why Holly's innocent statement should have such a permanent ring. 'Well, I'll look after them, you can be sure of that. And if I could get you a new pair——'

'Ain't no need for that,' retorted Samuel ungraciously, slipping the bit between Trader's teeth. 'You riding Athena, is that right? That's Miss Holly's horse. I generally ride Trader.'

'Do you?' Morgan eyed the stallion without affection. It was much bigger than the mare, it was true, but so far as he was concerned even the mare was a doubtful proposition. 'Well, I'm afraid it's years since I was on a horse of any kind, and quite honestly I'm not looking forward to riding either.'

Samuel snorted, but happily Holly reappeared just then, her hands pushed into her pockets, her breasts bouncing provocatively as she sauntered across the yard.

'Are you ready?'

'As I'll ever be,' responded Morgan, taking the reins Samuel offered to him, and swinging himself up on to the mare's back. 'So far, so good. Are you sure you're going to be all right?'

'On Trader?' Holly smiled at Samuel and swung herself up on to the stallion's back without effort. 'I gather Sam's been telling you he usually rides him. Well, he does. But only because his legs are longer.'

Morgan shrugged, adjusting himself more comfortably in the saddle. Already the slight exertion required to mount the animal and keep it under control was bringing out a film of sweat all over his body, and he thought the silk shirt he had been compelled to wear might really have to be abandoned.

After assuring herself that he was not a complete

novice, Holly led the way out of the yard and on to a grassy track that angled away from the house. Keeping the stallion on a firm rein, she kept their pace to a sedate canter, glancing around from time to time to ascertain that her companion was not in any difficulty. Morgan didn't altogether enjoy the feeling of being at a disadvantage, and it didn't help when Athena became skittish and started to chew on the bit.

'You're holding the reins too tightly,' said Holly, over her shoulder, and Morgan's mouth compressed. 'Just take it easy. She won't run away with you. You're handling her like an unbroken filly.'

Her tone was condescending, and Morgan guessed she was enjoying her moment of glory. On horseback, she was obviously in control, and he wondered if he had been wise to agree to this excursion.

They had entered a tunnel now, cut between towering walls of vegetation. The horses' hoofs crunched over a carpet of rotting stalks, and all around them the evidence of what had once been a thriving plantation fell into decay. Canes, which had once soared between ten and twenty feet into the sky, had gone to seed, and the weeds that grew between them had created a rank wilderness of plant and parasite alike.

'Depressing, isn't it?' said Holly, half turning in the saddle to look at him. 'Would you believe hundreds of slaves used to work in these fields? I used to think I could feel the atmosphere when I rode through here. A kind of anguish, or despair; the hopelessness of knowing there was no escape.'

Morgan inclined his head. 'It's a fanciful notion.'

'Maybe.' Holly was defensive. 'But I wouldn't like to ride here after dark.'

'Nor would I,' agreed Morgan fervently. 'Though not for the same reasons, I daresay,' he added, as Athena performed another crab-like manoeuvre.

Holly swung round again, evidently assuming he was making fun of her, and Morgan sighed. He hadn't intended to hurt her feelings. In all honesty he was interested in learning about the island. It was simply that he would have preferred to make the tour in the buggy. The one Holly had used to go to Charlottesville the previous day.

Holly had reached a gate and leaned down to unlatch it, leading the way into a yard, surrounded by the burnt-out shells of wood and tar-paper shacks. 'These were the slave quarters,' she said, as Morgan came up beside her. 'They were destroyed by my great-great-great-great-grandfather, I believe.' She grimaced. 'I'm never absolutely sure how many greats there should be.'

'But an ancestor of yours anyway,' murmured Morgan gently, looking around, and Holly nodded.

'Of my mother's,' she appended pointedly, and Morgan conceded the point before sliding down from the mare's back.

Even after only fifteen minutes in the saddle, his spine was aching, and he put his hands in the small of his back and stretched his stomach muscles. His rump, too, felt as if it had been systematically beaten, and he grimaced at the prospect of further punishment.

One or two of the cabins were still standing, roofless perhaps, but capable of revealing the cramped conditions their occupants had suffered. Leaving Holly sitting on her horse, Morgan ventured through the doorway of one of the shacks, his nose twisting ruefully at the unpleasant smell of damp and decay.

She was right, he thought, standing in the middle of what had once been both living and sleeping quarters. There was an atmosphere here. It was the desperate influence of suffering humanity, the pain and humiliation of years of oppression.

As he stood there, absorbing this revelation, he heard

the sound of a pipe being played. It was an eerie sound, its reed-like resonance echoing around the deserted buildings, evoking instinctively an image of the past. The haunting notes were not European in origin; they had a different intonation. It was the kind of music that had its roots in a darker continent, and with a flash of intuition Morgan guessed who was playing it.

He was not surprised to find that both Holly and her horse had disappeared. He wondered that she had left Athena to give him any comfort. As her intention had obviously been to scare him, she might easily have hidden the mare as well.

But a secondary consideration amended this impression. She no doubt had no desire to be caught; and if she had taken the mare away, how could she have explained her absence? As it was, she could pretend she had ridden on, and then, discovering he wasn't with her, had ridden back to find him. As she knew the area so much better than he did, it would be a simple matter for her to circle the cane-fields, and then ride back as if she had never taken a detour.

The piping had ceased when he emerged from the cabin, and Morgan realised he didn't have much time if he wanted to outwit her. The simplest solution would be to hide, so that when she came back she wouldn't be able to find *him*, and his lips parted delightedly at the prospect of her confusion.

Athena was not too overjoyed at being tethered behind another of the shacks, and she whinnied in protest when a broken spar of wood scraped her flank. 'I'm sorry, old girl,' Morgan muttered apologetically. 'But you want to be on the winning side, don't you? Even if Holly is your mistress.'

Morgan took up his position inside one of the burnt-out huts and, as he did so, another idea occurred to him. A sooty smear he had collected on his arm

suggested another way he might be able to turn the
tables, and with a mocking smile he daubed some of the
charcoal on his face.

As he had anticipated, Holly reappeared a few
minutes later, riding into the yard with the unmistakable
appearance of someone well-pleased with herself.
Morgan, viewing her approach through a crack in the
cabin wall, saw her confidence waver a little when she
found Athena had disappeared, but she dismounted
anyway, and looked doubtfully around the enclosure.

'Morgan!' she said, soothing Trader with a palm to his
nose. 'Mr Kane! Where are you? Did you lose your way?'

Morgan didn't answer. It was not part of his plan
that he should walk out into the sunlight where Holly
could plainly identify him. He wanted her to come
looking for him. Then they would see who found the
situation so funny.

His shoulder brushed against the wall of the hut and
he froze. He had taken off his shirt because its
whiteness was too revealing, and the scraping sound
seemed as loud as the piping had done earlier.

'Morgan?' Holly moistened her lips and looked in his
direction. 'Morgan, are you in there? What have you
done with Athena?'

He knew she couldn't see him by the uncertainty in
her step, and he felt sure she would have brought
Trader with her if she had thought she could get him
into the hut. Her face was flushed, and strands of silky
gold hair were escaping from the barrette she had
secured at her nape. She looked as anxious as she
obviously felt, and Morgan was half inclined to
abandon his ruse and save her any embarrassment.

'Morgan, can you hear me?' As she neared the hut,
Holly spoke again, but Morgan's urge to confess his
whereabouts disappeared at her words. 'Morgan, I
thought you were with me, honestly. It wasn't until I'd

gone about half a mile that I looked back and saw you weren't there. I naturally assumed you were following.'

Even then, he thought she was only half convinced he might be hiding. She had evidently decided to assure herself the hut was empty, but her real attention was elsewhere. Perhaps she thought he had taken fright and ridden back to the house. Probably that had been her intention. If he had abandoned the outing, he could hardly blame her if she wasted the rest of the morning looking for him.

She came out of the sunlight into the shadowy confines of the shack, and her eyes could not have adjusted before he rose up in front of her. No doubt if he had given her time to get her bearings, his plan would not have worked so successfully. As it was, a combination of her impediment and the charcoal he had smeared upon his body—added to a lingering sense of the supernatural—created a situation where anything was possible.

Her scream of terror was not feigned, and Morgan immediately regretted what he had done. It had been intended as a joke, that was all; a way to repay her for the trick she had attempted to play on him; but her response only left him feeling a heel. However, before he had a chance to voice his protest, she had fled, and he knew he had to catch her before she reached the stallion.

He charged out into the sunlight, an incongrous sight in Samuel's cut-down jeans and little else, his face and arms and chest all smeared with the blackening charcoal. 'Holly!' he yelled fiercely, as she dashed across the yard, and the urgency in his voice almost panicked the stallion. But it did, at least, have the desired effect. Holly stopped in her tracks and turned disbelievingly to face him, and Morgan halted, too, as he gave a rueful smile.

'You!' she said, incredulously at first, and then, as she realised she had been duped, her expression changed. 'You—you *bastard*!' she choked, clenching her fists. 'You filthy, rotten bastard!'

'Well, filthy, perhaps,' Morgan was agreeing drily, surveying the dirt streaked on his arms, when she flew at him, her fists flailing wildly. A stream of profanities spilled from her lips as she fought with him, using both her hands and her feet to good advantage, and Morgan winced in protest when one particularly well-aimed punch struck home.

'You,' he told her, fending her off, 'you started it!' And as she continued to batter him with her fists, he added infuriatingly, 'And where did you pick up that vocabulary? I thought well-brought-up young ladies didn't know such words.'

'You *pig*——'

'Better!'

'I hate you!'

'You hate being caught out,' corrected Morgan, at last succeeding in capturing her wrists and forcing them behind her back. 'I guessed what you were doing immediately. You should have been a musician. I quite enjoyed the recital.'

Holly surged angrily towards him. 'You think you're so clever, don't you?' she snarled, and he felt the sudden thrust of her breasts against his chest. The nipples were aroused and hard, barely concealed by the thin cotton vest she was wearing—and unintentionally provocative.

Morgan's stomach muscles clenched. Her aggressive stance had brought the lower half of her body into contact with his hips and, as he continued to hold her, he felt a wave of heat envelop his loins.

In spite of what Alison had said, he would never have believed he could be affected in this way by a girl less than half his age. But he was; and his first instinct was to thrust her away from him, and himself away from temptation. But, as if sensing the change in his reaction, Holly looked up at him at that moment, and the brilliant indigo eyes caught and held his unwilling gaze.

Immediately, her struggles ceased, and the arms he was using to control her became an unnecessary shackle. But he didn't let her go. When he released her wrists it was only to put his hands on the narrow bones of her hips, and although he knew he would bitterly regret it later, he couldn't prevent the urge to pull her fully against him.

'Morgan,' she breathed unsteadily, her freed hands sliding sensuously up his arms, and for the first time in his life, he lost his head. Without stopping to think of the consequences of his actions, without giving a thought to the inevitable result of his recklessness, he bent his head and covered her mouth with his own.

CHAPTER FIVE

HOLLY stood on the verandah, her hands thrust deeply into the pockets of her trousers, gnawing anxiously at her bottom lip. It was half past three and there was still no sign of Morgan. He should have been back by now. Even allowing for the fact that he didn't know the area, it simply wasn't possible to get lost for long. Besides which, Trader knew his way home. If there had been an accident, surely the stallion would have found his way back. But the fact remained, he hadn't, so what did it mean?

Samuel was out searching for him. She had wanted to go herself, but Lucinda wouldn't let her. 'That boy knows every inch of the plantation,' she had declared severely, when Holly protested. 'And if something has happened—the Lord forbid—what use would you be in getting Mr Kane back to the house?'

Holly knew she was right, but that didn't make the waiting any easier. Samuel had been gone over an hour already, and her nerves were beginning to shred. She could not dislodge the fear that anger might have made Morgan reckless. And he had been angry when he left her. She knew that only too well.

She shook her head. She should have been feeling pleased with herself for the way things had worked out, but this particular eventuality was something she had not bargained for. When Morgan took her in his arms and kissed her, she had known an overwhelming sense of achievement. But subsequent developments had rather overshadowed her success.

She sighed. At the time she had not really thought

much about her success, or the lack of it. In all honesty, when Morgan's mouth touched hers, she had been assailed by other emotions, and she had to admit revenge had not been one of them.

His mouth had been so disturbingly sensual, his hands in the small of her back so excitingly possessive. She had been pressed close against his lean, taut body, his sweat-moistened skin slick beneath her hands. She had wanted him to go on kissing her, not just to endorse her victory, but because she had been enjoying it. It wasn't the first time she had been kissed, but it was the first time she had felt her senses swimming, and when his hands had cupped her buttocks and brought her fully against his hard arousal, she had wanted nothing so much as for him to finish what he had started.

But it hadn't worked out like that—which was probably just as well, she reflected ruefully. If he had made love to her she was not at all sure she could have sustained her indifference to him. He wasn't like the young men she had known, none of whom had even tempted her to abandon her principles. Morgan was different. With him, she had known a disturbing loss of identity. And when he had thrust his forceful tongue into her mouth, she had quickly learned the dangers of playing with fire.

Holly shifted uneasily now, aware of an unwelcome ache between her thighs. He hadn't made love to her; that particular hazard had been avoided, so why did she feel so unsettled? To her good fortune—and, no doubt his—he had evidently remembered his duty to her father and he had thrust her away from him with a very uncomplimentary use of force. Before she had even regained her balance, Morgan had strode across to the nervous stallion, and swung himself up on to its back. And although she had recovered herself sufficiently to offer a word of protest, the savagery in his face had deterred a stronger plea.

By the time she had summoned up enough courage to search the ruined shacks in search of Athena, Morgan had disappeared, and, realising the mare was no competition for the powerful beast he was riding, Holly had eventually ridden back to the house.

That had been more than four hours ago, she estimated now, glancing at her watch. Of course, at first she had not been alarmed, even though she knew Trader bore no comparison to the kind of hacks used for pony-trekking. Morgan had seemed quite at home with Athena, and she had had no reason to believe he would not return for lunch. It wasn't until one o'clock came, and half-past, and then two o'clock, that she became anxious, and Lucinda remarked, with her usual candour, that something was definitely wrong.

Holly paced across the verandah now, for once finding no consolation in the view. She was tense, and worried—more worried than she wanted to be, she had to admit—and she prayed with all her heart that Lucinda was wrong.

Unable to stand her isolation any longer, Holly entered the house and walked reluctantly into the kitchen. She had been avoiding the housekeeper's company for two reasons: one, she didn't care to listen to Lucinda's predictions of gloom; and two, she had thus far evaded any questions over why Morgan should have been riding the stallion when he set out on the mare.

'No news?' Holly murmured now, lounging on to the bench beside the pinewood table, and Lucinda regarded her dourly.

'Oh, yes,' she said sardonically. 'He arrived back fifteen minutes ago, and I sent him upstairs to take a shower!' Her dark eyes flashed with impatience. 'What d'you take me for, girl? Do you think if I had heard something I wouldn't have let you know?'

Holly grimaced. 'There's no need to bite my head off.'

'Isn't there?' Lucinda snorted. 'Seems to me there's every need. A man doesn't disappear like that, not without a reason. And you coming back here covered in soot!'

Holly felt her colour deepening. 'I told you. We went into the old slave village. I must have brushed against one of the walls.'

'You must have sat down in it, too,' retorted Lucinda shortly. 'It was all over the seat of your trousers. If I was a suspicious woman, which I'm not, I'd be wondering if there wasn't some connection between your appearance, and Mr Kane's *dis*appearance!'

Holly sighed. 'Don't be silly, Luci.'

'All right.' The housekeeper opened the door of the fridge and took out a jug of orange juice. 'But I hope for your sake that he's all right. I shouldn't like to be in your shoes, if your Daddy has to be told his assistant has gone missing!'

'Oh, Luci!' Holly hunched her shoulders. 'How can he have gone missing? The island's not big enough.'

'That animal he's riding ain't trustworthy,' retorted Lucinda depressingly. 'And who knows what it might do with an inexperienced horseman on its back.'

'Luci!'

'Well.' The housekeeper shrugged. 'That cliff over at Angel's Point ain't that far away——'

'Luci, stop it!'

Holly started to put her hands over her ears to shut out the black woman's words when she heard the unmistakable sound of a horse's hoofs in the yard.

'They're here!' she exclaimed, leaping to her feet and beating the housekeeper to the door. But when she burst out of the house it was to find only Samuel, climbing down from the mare, though the stallion, too, was kicking its heels at the other side of the yard.

Immediately, she felt as if someone had given her a punch in the stomach, and she turned to the boy speechlessly, her expression eloquent of her feelings.

'I found him,' said Samuel flatly, looking beyond the girl to where his mother was leaning against the door. 'Where's Pa? I'm going to need him.'

Holly swallowed convulsively. 'He's not—he's not——'

'Hurt, yes. Dead, no,' responded Samuel shortly. 'Look, I don't have time to stand here discussing it. He'll be okay if I can get him back to the house.'

Holly spread her hands. 'Oh, God! Trader threw him!'

'It ain't Trader's fault,' retorted the boy impatiently. 'Miss Holly, you're not making things any easier for him by standing here asking me questions. The man's in pain. We've got to deal with it.'

'I'll come with you,' said Holly at once, but Lucinda at last intervened.

'Ain't no use you going with Samuel,' she exclaimed impatiently. 'You don't know nothing about first aid. Well? Do you?'

'I'm not helpless,' retorted Holly defensively. 'Where is he, Sam? Can I get the buggy to him?' She looked at Lucinda. 'You know Micah's away for the day, fishing. It's going to take ages to get him back.'

Samuel looked hesitant. 'Maybe you could get the buggy near enough for me to drag Mr Kane to it,' he murmured consideringly. 'I'd forgotten Pa wasn't here. Looks like you and me will have to manage, after all.'

'Now, wait a minute.' Lucinda stepped between them. 'How do you know you won't be hurting Mr Kane more than he is already by dragging him across the ground? Seems like he should see a doctor first. Samuel, where is he? Can you tell Holly how to find him?'

'Well—yes——'

'Then go on. Do it. She can go get Doc Harding, and you and me will go and see what we can do to help Mr Kane meanwhile.'

'But Luci——' Holly was seething with suppressed emotion. 'Doc Harding's house is ten miles away!'

'All the more reason for you not to be wasting time,' responded Lucinda flatly. 'Samuel and I will go in the buggy. You take the car.'

'Oh, Luci!'

'You're wasting time,' the black woman reminded her drily. 'And heaven knows we may not have it in a case like this.'

'A case like this!' Holly gasped, and turned to Samuel. 'For goodness sake! Is he unconscious?'

Samuel's shoulders sagged. 'I guess so,' he muttered, giving his mother a rueful look. 'Seems like he cracked his head when he fell.'

'Fell?' Holly knew she should be on her way, but anxiety kept her riveted to the spot. 'I thought you said it wasn't Trader's fault.'

'Mr Kane shouldn't have been riding him,' said Samuel impatiently. 'And if Trader had done something bad, he wouldn't have been hanging around, waiting for Mr Kane to get up. My guess is Mr Kane was riding too fast through the trees, and hit a low-hanging branch. There was plenty of them thereabouts, and that would account for the cut on his head.'

Holly stared at him. 'His head's cut?'

'A bit.' Samuel looked uncomfortable. 'Look—can we get moving? That ground is damp.'

Holly felt sick. 'What ground? Where is he?'

'Over by Stumper's Cove,' said Samuel unwillingly, naming a remote area north of the plantation, where a clump of mangroves made riding hazardous. 'I guess he must have taken the old trader's route past the slave village.'

'Oh, God!' Holly was aware that Lucinda was looking at her now, and she felt her colour deepening. 'He—he could be bleeding to death, and we're just wasting time talking about it.'

'I'll get some blankets,' said Lucinda at once, turning away towards the house. 'You get going, Holly. Like you said, he could be bleeding to death.'

It took only a few minutes to get the old saloon out of the stable that served as a make-shift garage. Although the ancient Packard had seen better days, Micah made sure it was always roadworthy, and he and Lucinda often used it when they went shopping in Charlottesville. Holly seldom drove the cumbersome old vehicle. She preferred the buggy, with its easier manoeuvrability, and it took her several minutes to get accustomed to having no gears.

Doc Harding's house was situated mid-way between the plantation and Charlottesville, and as she drove Holly prayed he would be there. He had a surgery in town and, since his wife died some years ago, he had taken to spending less and less time at the house. Holly knew he was acquiring the reputation of being something of a drinker, and he was often to be found in the Planter's Hotel on Broad Street, drowning his troubles—and his skill—in the island's favourite spirit.

The house certainly looked deserted as she turned between the gates, and Holly's heart sank. The place looked so dilapidated these days, and she wondered how the late Mrs Harding would feel if she could see its creeper-hung walls and peeling paintwork. One could not neglect one's property in this climate, as Holly had learned to her cost, and the jungle-like growth, that had once been hacked away with machetes, was gradually regaining ground.

Holly parked the Packard on the drive at the side of the house and, sliding out, walked round to the rear of the building. If Doc Harding was at home, he was more likely to be found on the verandah at the back of the house than sitting in state in one of the drawing rooms Mrs Harding had so immaculately furnished. Since his wife had died, he seemed to find his home claustrophobic, and Holly had once overheard Micah telling Lucinda that he had been known to sleep outdoors, too.

Bella, the mulatto woman the doctor had taken on as his housekeeper, was the only occupant of the verandah just now, Holly saw as she turned the corner. Seated in an old bamboo rocker, she was dozing the afternoon away, and Holly guessed that, without supervision, Bella was unlikely to show any enthusiasm for work.

Her sandals rang as she mounted the verandah steps, and Bella's eyes flicked open in alarm. 'Why—it's Miss Forsyth, isn't it?' she exclaimed, blinking up at the unsmiling girl. 'You startled me half to death! I thought it was Mr Simon, back already.'

'Mr Simon?' Briefly, Holly was diverted. 'You mean Dr Harding?'

'No. Mr Simon,' said Bella, getting to her feet and stretching luxuriously. 'Course, he's Doc Harding, too. But I couldn't call him that, could I? Not two of them!'

Holly shook her head. 'I'm afraid I don't understand, but I've not got the time to worry about that now. Where is the doctor? I must see him immediately.'

'Didn't I say?' Bella grimaced and began to amble along the verandah towards the kitchen door. 'Mr Simon's gone looking for him. Left about—I don't know—maybe half an hour ago. Should be back soon, though.' She glanced at the girl. 'You want some lemonade while you wait?'

Holly sighed. 'Who is Mr Simon?'

'I thought you knew.' Bella paused and tilted her head expectantly. 'That sounds like them now. I better go and make some strong black coffee. I guess the doc is going to need some.'

Holly's spirits swooped, but although she started after the housekeeper, she halted uncertainly when the sound of an approaching vehicle came to her ears. Apparently someone was back, and she could only hope the doctor was capable of understanding her.

The screech of brakes and the slamming of doors brought her to the rail at the side of the verandah, just in time to see two men covering the gravelled path towards her. One was Doc Harding obviously, but he was evidently in some distress. He was leaning heavily on the man supporting him, and as they drew closer, Holly could hear the garbled words he was trying to express.

'No need for you to come after me,' he was mumbling, with some indignation. 'I'd have come home—all in good time. Nothing for me here now, don't you know? I never asked you to be my keeper.'

His companion would have replied, Holly felt sure, but he looked up and saw her hanging over the rail and his expression changed. The scowl that had marred his pale, good-looking features disappeared, and he pushed his horn-rimmed spectacles up his nose with his free hand to give her a perplexed, but friendly, grimace.

'Can I help you?' he asked, and the older man blinked and looked up at her, too.

''S Holly,' he said, struggling to pull himself upright. 'You waiting for me, Holly? Is there something wrong?'

Holly stepped back as they came up on to the verandah, Doc Harding grasping the handrail and freeing himself from the younger man's support. Although he was endeavouring to appear in command of his actions, it was obvious the doctor was much the worse for drink, and Holly gazed at him helplessly, not knowing how to answer.

'I would assume your visitor came in search of your professional services, Uncle,' remarked the younger man drily. 'Can I help you, Miss—Holly? I'm a doctor, too. Dr Harding, also, for my sins!'

Holly was waiting by the kitchen door when the doctor's station wagon swept into the yard. It was closely followed by the buggy but Holly paid it little attention. She had seen Morgan, stretched out on blankets in the back of the doctor's vehicle, and her knees shook uncontrollably as she hurried out of the house.

'You keep out of the way, Holly,' ordered Lucinda, herself emerging from the back of the station wagon. 'Samuel and the doctor are capable of carrying Mr Kane into the house. You got his bed all turned down and ready? Good. Now, you go and put the kettle on. We may be needing some hot water bottles.'

'Hot water bottles?' echoed Holly blankly, trying to catch a closer glimpse of Morgan over Lucinda's unyielding shoulder. 'Is he all right? Is he still unconscious? Luci—you've got to tell me! I've been almost——'

'He's going to be all right.' It was the younger Dr Harding who answered her, coming round to the rear of the vehicle to open up the doors. 'But he's chilled to the bone, and there's always the danger of pneumonia. I suggest you do as Mrs Fletcher says and leave his immediate care to us.'

Holly swallowed her indignation and made a helpless gesture. What could she do, after all? she reflected. It wasn't as if she had any first aid training even. That was one thing the expensive finishing school had not covered.

Nevertheless, she was grateful for the reassuring smile Simon Harding cast in her direction. He really had proved to be a tower of strength, and without his intervention, she didn't know what she would have done. His uncle had been in no fit state to attend to anyone, and she had been unutterably grateful when Simon had offered his services. It turned out that he used to spend his holidays on the island, too, though he was some years older than Holly and therefore never a part of her scene. However, he did know Stumper's Cove as well as she did, and it had been at his suggestion that she came straight back to the house to prepare for the patient's arrival.

The waiting had seemed endless, and with darkness falling Holly had begun to fear the worst. But they were back now, she told herself fiercely, trying not to think how long Morgan might have been lying unconscious, and she held herself stiffly in control as Samuel and Simon Harding carried him into the house on a make-shift stretcher.

To her relief, his eyes were open now, though he was very pale and there was a bandage circling his head. However his lips parted wryly when he caught sight of Holly's agonised face. 'I told you I was no good with horses,' he murmured, his grey eyes dark with fatigue, and she was relieved that he didn't seem to remember the reason he had been riding Trader.

'Are—are you all right?' she stammered huskily, but before he could answer, they had transported him through the kitchen and into the hall beyond.

'You got that kettle on yet?' asked Lucinda sharply, bringing up the rear, and Holly flushed.

'Yes,' she said defensively, gesturing towards the stove, and Lucinda nodded.

'I'll be back in a few minutes, after I see what's needed,' she averred, bustling after the men, and Holly slumped down on to the bench by the table, feeling completely useless.

Samuel's appearance in the doorway gave her some respite, and she lifted her head to look at him. 'Is he going to be all right?' she asked, unable to wait until Lucinda was prepared to enlighten her, and the boy shrugged.

'I don't think it's anything serious,' he replied after a moment. 'The doc did say there was some swelling at the base of his spine, but he doesn't seem to be paralysed or anything.'

'Paralysed!' Holly was horrified. 'You mean—he could be?'

'No.' Samuel hunched his shoulders. 'Aren't you listening to me, Miss Holly? I said he's not paralysed. He can move his legs. The doc checked that out.'

Holly swallowed. 'And was he conscious—when you got to him, I mean?'

'Only just.' Samuel grimaced. 'I think he was still in a state of shock. You know—what with passing out and everything.'

'Hmm.' Holly cupped her chin on one hand, and expelled a heavy sigh. 'Oh, Lord! It's all my fault! If he really has hurt himself, my father's going to hit the roof!'

'And is that all that matters to you, young lady? What your father will say?' Lucinda's reappearance, carrying the blanket they had used to wrap Morgan in while he was lying on the ground, caused Holly no small discomfort. But she looked at the housekeeper defensively, hoping Lucinda had not heard everything she had said, and the black woman clicked her tongue with some impatience. 'It's lucky for you Mr Kane ain't seriously hurt,' she declared, bundling the dirty blanket into the washing machine. 'Encouraging him to ride that animal! In heaven's name, were you hoping he'd break his neck?'

No.' Holly was mutinous. 'And I didn't encourage him to ride Trader. He—he just took off on him.' She paused, and then added weakly, 'I—suppose he wanted to see what it was like.'

'You expect me to believe that?' Lucinda was scathing. 'What really happened out there? That's what I'd like to know. Must have been something for him to ride off and leave you!'

Holly shrugged. 'We—we had a difference of opinion,' she mumbled reluctantly, avoiding the housekeeper's knowing gaze. 'As you might have expected. I didn't exactly invite him here, did I?'

Lucinda regarded her for several seconds longer, and then abandoned her efforts. For the moment she had enough to do, coping with the doctor's demands, but Holly knew better than to suppose she had heard the last of it.

For the next half hour, the housekeeper was kept busy, running up and downstairs with cups of tea and hot water bottles, helping Simon Harding make his patient comfortable. The ugly gash on Morgan's temple had to be cleansed and re-dressed; several other cuts and bruises had to be attended to; and there were soiled dressings to remove, and blood-stained dishes to be sterilised; a hundred-and-one small duties to be attended to before the doctor came downstairs again.

By the time he did, Holly was tense and apprehensive, still not entirely convinced that Morgan was going to be all right. When she heard the heavier footsteps on the stairs, she came to the door of her father's study where she had been waiting, and without hesitation Simon Harding walked to meet her.

The lamps had been lit, but even in their warm glow Holly's face was still pale. Her eyes were wide and anxious, and there was a revealing tremor about her lips. The fears she had been endeavouring to bank down were still very much in evidence, and the young man felt his senses stir at her unguarded vulnerability.

'Is he going to be all right?'

Although she had already asked that question of both Samuel and Lucinda, Holly couldn't prevent the words tumbling from her tongue. She had to have his reassurance, the reassurance of someone with first-hand knowledge of Morgan's condition, and Simon gave her a gentle smile before stepping past her into the room.

'Do you think I could have a drink?' he suggested, nodding towards the tray still residing on the cabinet, and Holly quickly gathered her wits.

'Of course,' she said, walking stiffly across the room. 'What would you like? Rum? Whisky? Sherry?'

'Just a can of Coke, if you don't mind,' Simon responded easily, following her. 'Yes. That's fine. It doesn't matter if it's not chilled.'

The Coke looked unpleasantly warm, but Simon didn't seem to mind. He swallowed half the contents of the can at a gulp and then, wiping his mouth on the back of his hand, he surveyed her with calm deliberation.

'He's comfortable,' he said, indicating that she should sit down, but Holly was too tense to relax.

'Comfortable?' she echoed. 'What does that mean? Is he going to be all right or isn't he? Samuel said something about your being concerned about paralysis. There—there's no fear of that, is there?'

Simon considered for a moment, and then shook his head. 'No,' he said finally. 'No, I'm pretty sure that's not a problem we're going to have to deal with. I suppose Samuel was referring to the fact that there is some swelling around the spinal area. As far as I can ascertain at the moment, that's all it is—swelling. A natural result of his fall, wouldn't you say? That cove is honeycombed with exposed roots. My guess is he injured both his head and his back by falling on them.'

Holly nodded. 'And—and when will you know for sure?'

'Whether the swelling means anything more serious?' He shrugged. 'About a week, I guess.'

'A week!' Holly gulped. 'Ha—have you told—Mr Kane that?'

'I assume he knows,' remarked Simon drily. 'He's pretty stiff. I doubt if he'll even be able to get out of bed for the next few days. But as soon as he can, we'll take him into the hospital in Charlottesville for some X-rays.'

Holly caught her breath. 'I see.'

Simon frowned. 'You do realise Mr Kane won't be able to leave for at least ten days?' he exclaimed. 'I understand he works for your father. I think you should let him know.'

Holly nodded again. 'Yes. I think so, too.'

'Well ...' Simon smiled now. His professional mission accomplished, he evidently felt able to be more expansive. 'I hope I've been of some service.'

'Oh——' Holly lifted her head. 'You know you have. I—I don't know what I'd have done with your—your uncle——'

'... much the worse for wear,' filled in Simon drily, when she faltered. 'I know. The old man's just let things go since my aunt died. That's why I'm here. My father was concerned about him.'

Holly listened, trying to feign interest in the Hardings' affairs while her brain buzzed with the implications of what Simon had so casually related. Morgan was going to have to stay here, at least for another ten days. And although that might suit her purposes, she could well imagine how her father was going to react.

'I always liked the island,' Simon was saying now, and Holly made a concerted effort to concentrate on what he was saying. 'I may just decide to stay, after all. I know it's what my father is hoping for. But perhaps that's because he and my mother are hoping to retire here themselves in about five years.'

Holly blinked. 'You're—you're thinking of taking over your uncle's practice?' she ventured, realising she had not been paying attention, and Simon nodded.

'That's what I said,' he remarked ruefully. 'I guess you weren't listening. What's the matter? Don't you want an uninvited guest?'

'Oh, no.' Holly made a helpless gesture, realising her reactions could be misconstrued. 'I—er—it's just—I know Mr Kane will be expected back in London. He—he's my father's personal assistant, you see, and—well, he—my father, that is—isn't going to be very pleased.'

'Oh, I see.' Simon chuckled. 'You think your father's going to blame you. Well, I shouldn't worry about it. It's not as if Mr Kane isn't old enough to make his own mistakes. I daresay he's more concerned about what his wife's going to say. He is married, isn't he? I seem to recall him mentioning something about his sons.'

Holly's nerves tightened. 'He—he's divorced,' she answered quickly, twisting her hands together. 'I—is there anything special we should do to help him? I mean—I assume you want us to keep him in bed.'

'That shouldn't prove too much of a problem,' responded the doctor equably. 'Not in the immediate future, anyway. And don't worry. I'll be back to see him again in the morning. For tonight, I've given him a sedative, so he should sleep. Your housekeeper has my instructions. I don't think you'll find any difficulties. Mrs Fletcher seems perfectly capable of handling the situation.'

Holly silently agreed with him but, after he had gone, she couldn't resist the temptation to see Morgan for herself. After all, she had been instrumental in causing

his accident, however many excuses she might find for
herself.

Morgan was lying flat on his back when she tiptoed
into the bedroom. His eyes were closed, and the
lamplight cast hollowing shadows across his cheeks. The
bandage she had noticed earlier looked very white
against his hair, but less so against his skin. His usual
tan had abnormally receded, and even his lips had a
bluish tinge. Lucinda had obviously arranged the
bedding so that it covered his chest, but he had pushed
it back to his waist. In consequence, there was a
feathering of goose flesh across his body, which
contrasted sharply with the moistness of his skin. He
was sweating, yet he was shivering, too, and Holly's
hands trembled as she pushed them down the seams of
her trousers.

'What do you want?'

Morgan's enquiry set her nerves jangling, and she
saw to her dismay that his eyes were open now. His
earlier mockery, which might have been for Lucinda's
benefit, had quite disappeared, and his weariness was
palpable as he looked at her through narrowed lids.

'I—I came to see if—if there was anything I could
do,' she stammered awkwardly, moving towards the
bed. 'How do you feel? Are—are you in pain? Is there
anything I can get you?'

'Like a telephone?' enquired Morgan flatly. His
mouth compressed. 'How long am I supposed to stay
here?'

'I thought Dr Harding had told you.'

'No. He only said I should rest up for a couple of
days. Unfortunately, he does not know your father.
Where Andrew Forsyth is concerned, sprained backs
don't exist.'

Holly felt terrible. 'It's all my fault.'

'You could say that.' Morgan was dry. 'However,

you were not responsible for my ineptitude.' He closed his eyes for a moment and then opened them again. 'I must have been crazy!'

Holly licked her lips. 'You mean—you mean—to ride off on Trader?'

'That, too,' said Morgan grimly. 'But I was thinking of something else.'

Holly sighed. 'It's not important.'

'Oh, I agree!' Morgan was emphatic. 'However, it happened, and I have to deal with it.' His mouth tightened. 'I behaved like a fool, and there's no excuse for that. I'm sorry.'

Holly held up her head. 'It doesn't matter.'

'It does.' Morgan's lids sagged for a moment, then he forced his eyes open again. 'Damn Harding!' he muttered. 'Whatever it was he gave me is making my brain sluggish.' He blinked rapidly before adding, 'Before I flake out, you've got to promise me that you'll get in touch with your father. I was going to telex him myself tomorrow, but now I think you'd better use the phone. I assume there are phones in Charlottesville you can use.'

Holly shrugged. 'I suppose so.'

'What do you mean, you suppose so?' Morgan's eyes glittered for a moment, but he was growing weary. She could see it.

'I mean—we'll talk again in the morning,' said Holly, the anxiety that had been gnawing at her for the past few hours giving way to an unsteady sense of relief. Morgan was going to be all right. She was suddenly convinced of it. And, although she had her father's anger to face, she had been granted an unexpected term of reprieve.

CHAPTER SIX

HOLLY drove home from Charlottesville with a heavy heart. For once, she had not found solace in her work at the school, and even Paul Bergerac's clowning had not been able to lift the sense of depression that was gripping her. Stephen had been sympathetic, of course, but she could not confide her problems to him. In fact, all the members of the school staff had offered their commiserations to Morgan, and she could hardly complain about his continued presence when it wasn't his fault.

No, what troubled Holly most was the realisation that what had begun as a ploy to evoke her father's anger with Morgan was fast becoming something else. Since that fateful morning at the slave village, she was finding it increasingly difficult to understand her own feelings, and while she kept telling herself that nothing had changed, she knew it had.

Not that Morgan seemed to share her dilemma. On the contrary, since he had arrived on the island his attitude towards her had veered from studied tolerance to outright contempt, the latter culminating in the row they had had two days ago.

It had been her fault, of course. She had not done what he had asked her to do, and she had known that sooner or later she would be called to account. Even so, had not Lucinda chosen to play advocate, she might have been able to delay the evil day.

'Don't you think you ought to go and see the man?' she had argued the day after Holly was supposed to have spoken to her father on the telephone. 'I think you owe it to him to tell him exactly what your Daddy said, don't you?'

Holly was sitting on the verandah at the time, one bare foot resting on the slatted wood two steps down, her other leg hooked up in front of her to support the sketch pad she was using. She had been intent on her subject, the charcoal moving swiftly and surely across the paper, blocking out the insistent voice of her conscience. But Lucinda's intervention had been sharp and unannounced, and Holly started violently when the irate tones interrupted her.

Tilting her head mutinously, her thumb smudging the unwary stroke the housekeeper's question had instigated, Holly had endeavoured to maintain her independence. 'I'll see him later,' she answered carelessly, without looking up. 'Oh—and don't make me any lunch, will you? I'll just have a sandwich when I'm ready.'

'Will you?' Lucinda's disapproval was unmistakable and, in spite of her determination, Holly was disturbed. 'And just when is *later*, may I ask? Seems like you've been avoiding that man ever since you got back from town.'

Holly expelled her breath a little nervously. 'It's not your concern, Luci,' she retorted, hoping the housekeeper would go away, but Lucinda was not appeased.

'You ever think he might wonder if I'm giving you his messages?' she exclaimed fiercely. 'He's been asking to see you ever since I took in his breakfast this morning. You did do as he asked you, didn't you? You did tell your father about Mr Kane's accident?'

'Of course.' At last Holly was forced to meet the housekeeper's accusing eyes. 'I contacted Daddy, just as I said. Now, do you mind if I get on with my work?'

'Your work!' For once Lucinda was scathing of her talent. 'Don't you care that that man's lying there, worrying himself sick over all the time he's wasting? And you could ease his mind. But you won't.'

'Luci, I——'

'Don't you "Luci" me! There are times when I could take my slipper to you, Holly Forsyth, and this is one of them!'

'Oh, all right!' With a groan of frustration, Holly put her charcoal and the sketch pad aside and got abruptly to her feet. 'All right, all right, I'll talk to him. But don't blame me if your patient doesn't like what I have to tell him!'

Morgan's room had been pleasantly cool when she entered it a few minutes later. She came in from the upstairs balcony, aware that by doing so she had a momentary advantage. The sunlight behind her put her face into shadow and for a moment she could see him without him being able to see her.

He was lying flat on his back, just like the last time she had seen him. As before, his chest was exposed to the air, but this time cream cotton pyjama trousers covered his lower limbs. She guessed they belonged to her father. The ruching around his waist revealed that they were several sizes too large for his slim hips. The slit up the front gaped a little, too, but this was quickly remedied when he identified his visitor.

'Holly,' he greeted her drily, levering himself up on his elbows, and reaching for the sheet to cover him. 'So you did get back from Charlottesville. I was beginning to wonder.'

Holly moistened her dry lips, and then hurried to the bed, moving to adjust his pillows before he lay back. She had thought she might have exaggerated the sexual appeal of the man, but she hadn't. Just doing these simple tasks for him made her hands all clammy, and she wondered if what had happened between them was still in his mind, too.

Evidently, she was wrong. As she straightened up from the bed, his hand shot out to fasten round her wrist, but not with any trace of affection. His lean hard fingers bit almost cruelly into her flesh, and his tone was savage when he addressed her.

'Did you do it?' he demanded, his eyes almost black as they bored into hers. 'Did you speak to your father? Or is your unusual desire for reclusivity your way of hiding that you hadn't the guts?'

Holly caught her breath. 'Let go of me!'

'Not until you tell me what I want to know.' Morgan's mouth was an uncompromising line. 'If you haven't let your father know what's been going on, you may wish you'd kept out of my sight a little longer!'

Holly made a futile attempt to free herself, and then glared at him defiantly. 'And if I haven't?' she retorted, refusing to let him see he was hurting her. 'What can you do about it, *Mr* Kane? You're hardly in a position to force my hand.'

'You think not?' Without releasing her, Morgan swung his legs over the side of the bed, and dragged himself into a sitting position. Ignoring the sheen of sweat that had broken out on his forehead, he used her arm as a pivot to force himself to his feet. But although he gained a standing position, the effort was evidently too great, for he uttered a muffled groan and sank down on to the bed again, gritting his teeth against the strength it had cost him. This time, while he strove for breath, he had no awareness of the shortcomings of her father's pyjamas, and Holly's eyes darted swiftly away from the curls of dark hair they exposed.

'Christ!' Morgan muttered violently. 'What the hell has that fool Harding done to me?'

'It's more what you've done to yourself,' said Holly quietly, and as if only just realising she was with him,

Morgan freed her to grope impatiently at the opening of the trousers.

A faint thread of colour invaded his cheeks at the discovery of what had occurred, but his tone was as grim as ever, and he made no apology for his immodesty. 'Am I to take it you have not spoken to your father?' he enquired, pushing himself back against his pillows again with an obvious effort, and Holly sighed.

'I haven't—spoken to him, no,' she admitted, stepping back from the bed, just in case he attempted to pursue his anger. Then, before he could utter the imprecation she was sure was about to spill from his lips, she added quickly, 'But I did send him a telex. He knows what happened.'

Morgan's jaw was hard as he regarded her. 'I asked you to phone.'

'I know you did.' Holly lifted her shoulders. 'But I didn't want to.'

'Why?' Morgan's voice was bleak.

Holly licked her lips. 'I just didn't. It's not that important.'

'Isn't it?' Morgan dragged the sheet across his thighs. 'I think it is important. I think the reason you didn't speak to your father is quite simple to understand: you know why I'm here; and you're afraid that, if you speak to your father, he won't prove as easy to fool as me!'

Holly held up her head. 'I haven't fooled you.'

'Haven't you?' Morgan's lips twisted. 'You disappear for a whole day immediately after my arrival——'

'You know why. I have a job!'

'. . . you come on strong in the evening, so that I'll be forced to leave any discussions until the morning——'

'I did not come on strong!'

'. . . you steal my clothes——'

'I left you the towel!'

'. . . and finally, you create a situation for which your father would have put you over his knee!'

Holly gazed at him angrily. 'That's not fair!'

'What's not fair?' Morgan regarded her without liking. 'That ever since I arrived, you've done your best to make life difficult?'

Holly's jaw jutted. 'You kissed me, remember?' she reminded him indignantly, using the only weapon left to her, and Morgan's mouth drew into an ugly line.

'I wondered when we'd get around to that!' he said, his expression contemptuous. 'Yes. I kissed you, Holly—as any normal male would have done, confronted by a half-naked nymph who's been throwing herself at his head ever since he got here!'

Now Holly took the bend in the road before making the final descent through the derelict plantation. She was home earlier than usual, Stephen having offered to take her final class so that she could get away. She had been grateful. She had been finding it difficult to feel any enthusiasm for the lesson, and although she had little enthusiasm for returning home either, there was nowhere else to go.

She had not set eyes on Morgan since that angry exchange, and she didn't expect to. At first, she had not wanted to see him, humiliated beyond reason by his cruel denunciation. But gradually, the pain had eased, and with it her resentment, leaving a dull sense of apathy at the futility of her attempts to play with his emotions.

A telex had arrived from her father the day after their confrontation, but it had been delivered by Lucinda. Micah had picked it up from the Post Office in Charlottesville, and Holly had no way of knowing what it had contained. She had refused to ask the housekeeper. If Morgan wanted her to know, he would tell her. But, so far, she remained completely in the dark, and she consoled herself with the thought that what she didn't know couldn't hurt her.

When she reached the house, she parked the buggy in the yard as usual, before trudging into the kitchen. There was no one about so, slinging her holdall into a corner, she helped herself to a glass of iced fruit juice from the fridge. She was hot and sticky, and looking forward to the shower she intended to take—her only pleasure, it seemed, in a future that looked particularly bleak at this moment. She wished Morgan had never come here. She wished her father had simply sent her the air fare and ordered her back to London, as he had been known to do in the past. Then she would never have conceived the idea of seducing Morgan; then her own emotions would never have become involved.

Guessing the housekeeper was napping on the verandah, Holly left her holdall where it was and crossed the hall to the stairs. Lucinda would see the buggy when she woke up and surmise where her young mistress had gone. After she had a shower, she would make some tea, if the housekeeper was still sleeping. Perhaps, if she made a determined effort, she could shake off this feeling of depression once and for all.

She was tempted to peep into Morgan's bedroom before taking her shower, but the memory of that last encounter was not encouraging. Besides, Lucinda had confided that Morgan had spent a couple of hours downstairs the previous afternoon, while Holly was out, which seemed to confirm that he was still eager to avoid her. It was possible that he, too, was relaxing on the verandah at the moment, for she was not expected back for at least another hour. But the prospect of finding out, and maybe creating further animosity, was not appealing. She had the unpleasant suspicion that

Morgan was waiting until he was fit enough to make the journey before telling her his plans. Then, he would announce their departure forthwith, giving her no time at all to create any obstacles.

Now, Holly stripped off her shirt and the knee-length cotton shorts she had been wearing, closing her eyes for a moment as the warm air fanned her hot skin. Then, with a determined shrug of her shoulders, she walked into the bathroom, only to stop short at the sight of Morgan, sitting in the bath.

This time, she was as disconcerted as he had been when he found her in a similar position. The last place she had expected Morgan to be was in the bath, and she was not prepared for the flood of emotion that reddened her skin at his appearance. Thank God she was still wearing a bra and pants, she thought swiftly, though her lacy under-garments were scarcely adequate cover. Nevertheless, in her present frame of mind they provided a flimsy barrier to his frustrated gaze.

Morgan, for his part, was quite modestly concealed below the ring of soapy water. He had evidently washed his hair, for it was plastered close to his head, and drops of water trickled with unknowing sensuality down the muscled contours of his chest. Tiny globules of moisture trembled on the fine whorls of hair that arrowed towards his navel, drawing Holly's eyes downward, and although she knew she was inviting his censure, the inducement was irresistible.

'What are you doing here?' Morgan demanded wearily, interrupting her thought processes and dragging her attention back to his face. But, although she had anticipated his question, and the force of anger that should have accompanied it, Morgan's voice held only a degree of irritation, an almost studied acceptance that she should be the one to invade his privacy.

'I——'

'Did Lucinda send you?' he enquired, reaching for the thick turquoise towel draped over the curved shelf at the side of the bath. 'I thought she had more sense. I told her what I intended to do.'

Holly blinked. 'Lucinda?' She shook her head. 'I think Lucinda's probably dozing on the verandah.'

'That figures.' Morgan wiped the moisture from his face with the towel, his mouth drawing down at the corners. 'And I suppose you thought you'd try and shock me again. Well, forget it, Holly. I've seen you in the nude, remember?'

Holly's face burned. 'I'm afraid I don't know——'

'Oh, come off it!' Morgan spoke harshly. 'Why else would you come in here wearing something as revealing as that? You were hoping to make a scene, weren't you? Maybe you had some idea of using the housekeeper as a witness. Something to write home to Daddy about. Attempted rape? Was that what you had in mind?'

Holly gulped. 'How—how dare you?'

'Isn't it true?'

'Of course it's not true!' Holly fought for control as she turned towards the door. 'You have a twisted mind, Mr Kane! No wonder you and my father get along so well——'

'Wait!' As she reached the door to her room, his voice arrested her. 'Holly! Don't go.'

She didn't turn. 'Why not?'

'Because—well, because I didn't mean that.' He sighed. 'Maybe I've misjudged you. Maybe you didn't hear me.'

'Hear you?' Holly glanced at him over her shoulder. 'I didn't hear you in the bath, if that's what you mean.'

Morgan's shoulders sagged. 'How long have you been here?'

'You mean—back home?'

'That's right.'

'I don't know exactly.' She shrugged. 'Ten minutes. Fifteen, maybe. What does that matter?'

'It matters—because I have been shouting for assistance for the past three-quarters of an hour,' retorted Morgan heavily. 'I've been trying to attract someone's attention. I need Sam or Micah to help me out of the bath.'

Holly gripped the frame of the door with both hands as she looked at him. 'You mean—you can't get up?'

'Obviously not.' Morgan evidently resenting having to make the admission. 'Something's locked. When I try to move—well, I can't. I just need someone to help pull me up.'

Holly caught her lower lip between her teeth. The temptation to tell him it served him right after the way he had spoken to her was appealing, but his comments had not been that far off the mark. Only she had never thought of using Lucinda as a witness, which just went to prove she was not as cunning as she had thought.

'They say hot water weakens you,' she remarked now, consideringly, and saw the muscle tighten in his cheek.

'I don't really care what "they" say,' he responded bleakly. 'Just do me a favour and ask one of your employees to come up here. I'm persuaded that your friend Harding might know what he's talking about, after all.'

Holly frowned. 'Did Simon advise you not to take a bath?'

Morgan expelled his breath impatiently. 'Not in so many words. He said I should avoid too much exercise, that's all. I didn't know getting up out of a bath was energetic until now.'

Holly nodded. 'I see.' An unwarranted bubble of amusement was taking the place of her earlier resentment. 'No wonder you're so grumpy. It must be a new experience for you to find yourself in hot water!'

'Very funny.' Morgan's smile was scarcely humorous. 'Now will you do as I ask and call Sam or Mr Fletcher?'

Holly hesitated for a moment. Then she said flatly, 'I can't.'

'Why can't you?' Morgan's voice had an edge to it now.

'Because they're not here,' replied Holly reasonably. 'It's Thursday. Micah generally goes to Charlottesville on a Thursday.'

'And Sam,' prompted Morgan, between his teeth.

'I don't know where Sam is,' responded Holly, drawing her fingernail along the grain of the wood. 'At a guess, I'd say he's probably gone fishing. There's not much else to do here, once his chores are done.'

Morgan regarded her grimly. 'So what are you saying?'

Holly shrugged. 'I'm saying there's no one I can ask to help you. At least, not for another hour or so.' She straightened and turned back towards her bedroom. 'I guess I'll have to take my shower later. I don't think Lucinda would approve of us both sharing the bathroom at the same time.'

'*Holly!*' As she was disappearing into her room, Morgan's frustrated tones once again drew her attention. 'Holly, for God's sake!' he muttered. 'You can't just leave me here!'

Holly hesitated just inside her bedroom, and then turned and put her head round the door. 'What would you have me do?' she countered, adopting an innocent expression, and his eyes darkened angrily as he guessed she was enjoying his discomfort.

'You'll have to help me,' he gritted, making an abortive attempt to lever himself up, before sinking back, groaning, into the water. 'For pity's sake, Holly, you must have seen a naked man before. Just help me to get on my feet. I'll be okay, once I'm standing.'

Holly's tongue circled her lips. 'And what if Lucinda comes and sees us?' she ventured softly. 'Aren't you afraid of the interpretation she might put on me helping you? I mean—she might think you'd lured me into the bathroom.'

'All right, Holly, you've had your fun.' Morgan was keeping his temper with evident difficulty. 'Just go and put some clothes on, will you? If you went around decently clad like everyone else, the problem wouldn't arise.'

Holly arched one indignant brow. 'For someone in your position, you're remarkably arrogant——'

'Holly!'

'Oh, all right.' With a grimace, she capitulated, and turning back into the bedroom, she swiftly donned the shirt and shorts she had just discarded. Tying the ends of her shirt beneath her breasts for quickness, she sauntered back into the bathroom, her pace slowing instinctively as she approached the bath.

Morgan expelled his breath on a low sigh of relief, and stretched out his hand. 'If you can just help me to stand up, I should be able to make it,' he said. 'That's right. I'll try not to put my whole weight on you. *God*! I feel so bloody helpless! Who'd have thought a fall from a horse could create such havoc?'

'Anyone who knows horses would,' retorted Holly, avoiding looking at him. The hard strength of his arm about her shoulders was already causing her pulses to race, and as his lean body came up out of the water, the temptation to stare was almost irresistible.

Morgan panted a little as he gained his feet, and Holly reached for the towel and handed it to him. 'Thanks,' he said wrapping the concealing folds around him. 'And thanks for your help. I was pretty desperate.'

'You're not out of the bath yet,' Holly pointed out

huskily, aware that she was trembling. 'Do you want me to stay?'

Morgan's lips twisted. 'I don't think that will be necessary,' he responded, putting a hand in the small of his back and flexing the muscles experimentally. 'I think I can just about crawl out of here. But I don't know if I can make it downstairs, as I promised.'

Holly frowned. 'Promised? Promised who?'

'Your housekeeper,' replied Morgan drily, using the ends of the towel to wipe away the water dripping from his hair. 'Now, do you mind if I ask you to get lost? I've no desire for you to witness any further humiliation on my part.'

Holly hesitated. 'Are you—I—mean—well, do you have any idea when you might be—might be leaving?'

'Holly!' Morgan gazed at her impatiently. 'This is not the time or the place to discuss something like that.'

'I know.' She hunched her shoulders. 'But you don't talk to me.'

'Whose fault is that?'

Holly grimaced. 'I suppose you think it's mine.'

Morgan sighed, and then, steeling his expression, he levered his leg over the low rim of the bath. It obviously pained him, but he succeeded in completing the operation, and when he was standing beside the bath, he regarded her with some resignation.

'Harding says I can probably leave here in three or four days,' he told her flatly. 'I've telexed your father to that effect.'

Holly moistened her lips. 'And—and you expect me to—to go with you?'

Morgan sighed. 'It's what your father expects.'

Holly pursed her lips. 'And if I refuse?'

'I shouldn't.'

Holly sniffed. 'Are you threatening me?'

'No.' Morgan hesitated a moment longer, and then

began to move with some difficulty back to his room. 'No one can make you do what you don't want to do, Holly. You're over eighteen. You're not a minor any more——'

'But you think Daddy will make me, don't you?' she interrupted him frustratedly.

'I think he won't make it easy for you,' conceded Morgan, reaching his door, and briefly supporting himself against the frame. 'I suppose it all comes down to money in the end. Can you support yourself without his allowance?'

'Here?' Holly spread her hands. 'I suppose I could just about manage on what I earn from the mission.'

'And the horses? And this house? Not to mention the Fletchers,' inserted Morgan shrewdly, strangling Holly's tentative bid for freedom at birth.

'Oh, yes,' she exclaimed bitterly. 'He'd use them, wouldn't he?' She shook her head. 'I don't know how you can work for a man with so little compassion for his own flesh and blood!'

Morgan straightened. 'I don't deal in emotions, Holly. I deal in facts. And, right now, your father wants you back in London. Whether you go or not is up to you.'

CHAPTER SEVEN

IN fact, Morgan did come downstairs for dinner. By the time Holly had recovered herself sufficiently to put in an appearance, he was already seated behind her father's desk in the study, silently contemplating the dusty Bible which was open in front of him. To her surprise, he was wearing a loose-sleeved cotton shirt and narrow-legged cotton trousers, both of which she had not seen before. They were black, and the sombre colour suited his dark colouring, drawing attention to the swarthy cast of his skin and the pale grey brilliance of his eyes.

Something of her confusion must have shown in her eyes however, for he met her gaze only briefly before remarking casually, 'Micah got some things I wanted in Charlottesville. I didn't intend such a prolonged visit, as you know.'

Holly, conscious that in spite of her efforts her eyes were still swollen from the tears she had shed earlier, lifted her shoulders dismissively. 'It's nothing to do with me. But you could tell me what you're doing with that book. I don't believe my father's power of attorney gives you the right to poke about in private family records!'

'It doesn't, of course,' responded Morgan carelessly, but he made no attempt to close the Bible. 'However, after our visit to the plantation the other day, I was curious to learn about your ancestors. I've heard about records like these, but I've never actually seen one before. Did you know your birth was entered? And that of your mother?'

'My grandmother kept it up to date,' said Holly coldly, crossing the room and flipping the heavy volume shut. 'But I don't think she would approve of your motives, *Mr* Kane. As far as I know, she was one of only two people in the world who ever cared about me.'

'The other being——?'

'My grandfather, of course.' Holly gathered the heavy tome into her arms. 'Excuse me.'

Morgan sighed. 'Your father loves you, Holly,' he said levelly. 'You have to believe that.'

Holly winced. 'As you said earlier, *Mr* Kane, I'm not a child any more. I don't believe in fairy stories.'

'It's not a fairy story.' With an evident effort, Morgan thrust himself up from his chair, and followed her across the room to where she was restoring the Bible to its original position on the shelves. 'Holly, for God's sake, stop feeling so sorry for yourself!'

'Me?' She turned to gaze at him indignantly. 'Feeling sorry for myself?'

'Well, aren't you?' he retorted, supporting himself with a hand on either side of her.

'No, I——'

'You want your father to go on supporting you, but you don't want to give anything in return. Isn't that the truth?'

'Is that what my father says?'

'No, damn you, it's what I'm saying,' grated Morgan impatiently. 'When have you ever done anything that wasn't *self*-motivated?'

Holly gasped. 'Why you—you——'

'At a loss for words, *Miss* Forsyth?' Morgan gave a short mocking laugh. 'I seem to have drawn blood, don't I? Could it be that you actually recognise the truth when you hear it?'

Holly stiffened. 'If that's what you choose to believe, I can't stop you, can I?'

'Oh, Holly!' His harsh use of her name was raw with impatience. 'You've got to stop feeling that no one cares what happens to you. They do. Believe me!'

'Do you?'

The words were out before she could prevent them, and afterwards she tried to convince herself it was what she had intended. Certainly, Morgan did not believe her motives were as artless as they truly were, but just at that moment neither of them was particularly conscious of the other's interpretation. The question that had sprung so naturally to Holly's lips required an instant evaluation, and Morgan's involuntary reaction drove all other thoughts from their heads.

With a groan, half of anguish, half of protest, his hands moved to cradle her face between his palms. Then, the distaste he felt for his own actions crossing his face in a grimace of defeat, he put his thumbs beneath her chin and tilted her face to his.

His mouth was as hot and demanding as on that other occasion he had kissed her. Only this time she was prepared for him, and her lips parted instinctively to the hungry pressure of his. With his tongue tasting the tentative sweetness opened to him, Morgan had little strength left to sustain his present position. As the tremor in limbs still weakened by his condition got the better of him, he was forced to allow his body to rest heavily against hers. His chest crushed her breasts, the nipples hardening against his muscled flesh and, as his mouth continued its devastating possession she felt again the intimate thrust of his manhood throbbing between them.

'Do you want me?' Holly breathed, stifled by his weight and her emotions, and Morgan uttered a sound of self-disgust.

'Would there be any point in denying it?' he demanded, his breath moistening the curve of her ear.

He drew a harsh breath, and pushed himself back from her, his forehead beaded with sweat, 'It would serve you right if I took up your so-generous invitation! I realise it wouldn't be any novelty for you. You've probably had more men than my ex-wife, and that's saying something. But somehow, I don't think you're thinking of the pleasure we could give one another; only of how much leverage it would give you with your father!'

Holly wanted to slap his insolent face, but she was very much afraid that, if she did so, he would simply keel over under the blow. And, despite his scornful denigration, she found she couldn't deliberately hurt him. Not physically, at least.

Instead, she chose her words with care. 'What's the matter, *Mr* Kane?' she taunted bravely. 'Afraid of the competition?'

'Hardly,' he countered, refusing to respond in the way she had intended. He made his way with some difficulty to the desk and rested his hips upon it. 'It's something you learn with age, Holly. Discrimination. Yes, that's the word. And self-restraint; even in the face of extreme provocation!'

Holly slept badly that night, which was no novelty, either. Ever since Morgan's arrival she had been fighting the emotional upheaval his appearance had created, and now, more than ever, she was torn by her emotions. She told herself she hated him; that once again he had proved how unreliable he was; that he was her father's familiar and, as such, incapable of any decent feelings. But it didn't help. Deep down inside her, she could not destroy the faltering belief that he was not as black as he seemed and, although she knew it was a faint hope, she clung to this conviction.

She was due at the mission school that day and, as

she anticipated Morgan would spend the morning in bed, she saw no reason to alter her schedule. 'I'd have thought you'd want to be here when Doc Harding comes,' commented Lucinda sharply, serving her breakfast with a reproving air. She eyed the girl's much-depleted appetite with a jaundiced eye. 'Ain't no use you fretting none. After what you did, seems like you got no choice but to go back with Mr Morgan.'

'After what *I* did?' Holly was indignant. 'I didn't *do* anything.'

'I told you it wasn't no good running out on Mr Morgan,' continued Lucinda, almost as if Holly hadn't spoken. 'If'n you'd acted like an adult—if'n you'd sat right down with him and explained the reasons why you didn't want to go back to England, he might have been prepared to listen to you. But no. You had your own ideas about getting your own way. And where has it got you? Nowhere, that's what!'

Holly sighed. 'You don't understand, Luci——'

'I understand enough,' retorted the black woman. 'Mr Morgan—he told me how it is. Seems like your Daddy needs someone to take charge of his household, now that Mrs Forsyth has up and left him——'

'The *fourth* Mrs Forsyth!' put in Holly bitterly. 'Let's not forget the numbers.'

'All right.' Lucinda inclined her head. 'But that don't mean nothing. Maybe the poor man just ain't found anyone to take your poor Momma's place, that's all. You should be proud of that; not moaning about it.'

Holly pushed back the bench and got to her feet. 'I see *Mr* Morgan has convinced you anyway,' she declared unsteadily. 'But I'm still going to work, Luci. This may be the last chance I'll get.'

Stephen came to find her in the middle of the morning. Holly had taken her coffee outside, and was seated on the low stone wall that surrounded the play area, absorbed in the view and totally indifferent to the noise the children were making.

'I hear you may be leaving us, after all,' he said, causing her to look up at him almost blankly, her mind still occupied with the thoughts she had been nurturing.

'What? Oh—yes. Probably,' she responded dully, numb to any sympathy on his part. She had had to make the situation known to the Reverend Frost, and she guessed he had lost no time in telling one of the school's chief benefactors.

'I thought you were going to fight this,' protested Stephen, propping his hips against the wall beside her. 'Holly, you don't *have* to go. Oh, I know what you said about living in your father's house and so on, but you could find alternative accommodation——'

'It's not just the house,' said Holly flatly, 'If Daddy was to sell the old Gantry place, what would Micah and Lucinda do? Not to mention Sam, of course. And the horses. What about my horses? I couldn't let them be abandoned.'

'Horses survive,' said Stephen shortly. 'Human beings find it rather more difficult.'

Holly shook her head. 'I know you mean well, Steve——'

'. . . but you're leaving anyway.'

'I can't see any alternative.'

'But what about your painting? What about your art? Didn't you say your father always made it difficult for you?'

Holly gave him a rueful smile. 'I don't think my art would persuade him, do you? Let's face it, I'm not *that* good. I can daub a little, but that's all.'

Stephen's lips compressed. 'I assume this means your visitor has made a full recovery?'

'He's making it,' said Holly tersely, not wanting to

think, let alone talk, about Morgan Kane, but Stephen was not diverted.

'Harding says he's pretty tough,' he continued irritatingly. 'For a man of his age, that is. He's in his forties, isn't he?'

'He's forty-one,' retorted Holly, unknowingly revealing that she was not as indifferent as she would like to appear, and her companion frowned.

'How do you know?' he asked. 'Have you discussed his age? You seem very sure about something that's hardly relevant.'

'You brought it up,' Holly reminded him crossly, annoyed that she had unwittingly exposed her interest. Concentrating on the sails of the boats down in the small careenage, she hoped he would take the hint and leave. But Stephen was not finished yet.

'I wonder,' he said, with annoying insistence, and Holly was forced to turn and look at him again.

'What do you wonder?' she asked, barely able to keep the edge of frustration from her voice, and he shrugged.

'Maybe you're not so opposed to leaving now as you were,' he remarked broodingly. 'Who knows? Perhaps this man, Kane, has been more persuasive than I thought. What's he like? You said he was—nice. But what does that mean?'

Holly bent her head. 'Steve, please! You're being silly. As you've just pointed out, Morgan Kane is a man in his forties. What could he and I possibly have in common?'

'How about—Andrew Forsyth?' enquired a lazy voice behind her, and Holly turned with a start to find the man they had been discussing standing only an arm's length away. He was supporting his weight with the means of a narrow cane walking stick but, apart from this affectation, he looked perfectly well.

Stephen was even more taken aback than she was, Holly guessed, as he came abruptly to his feet to face the older man. Yet, although Morgan was older, the differences between them were more pronounced in their physical make-up than in their actual physical appearance. As Holly had once surmised, compared to Stephen's stocky build, Morgan had the grace and suppleness of a feline, though there was nothing remotely feminine in the lean, muscular strength of his body. It was obvious he was older, of course. It was there in the studied intelligence of his eyes, and in the lightly drawn lines that life's experiences had drawn on his face. But the comparisons between them merely made Stephen look that much younger, and anyone meeting them for the first time would be hard-pressed to decide how old Morgan actually was.

However, at the moment, Holly was more concerned with how much of their conversation he had actually heard. The noise the children had been making had deafened their ears to his approach. But Morgan had had time to overcome that obstacle, and Holly's voice was cold, though she made an effort to speak politely.

'What are you doing here?' she asked. She glanced about her in sudden confusion. 'How did you get here? Did Micah bring you?'

'Harding gave me a lift,' responded Morgan carelessly, his eyes on Stephen's vaguely aggressive face. 'He wanted to take some X-rays, remember?' He paused, and then added smoothly, 'I thought you might offer me a cup of coffee.'

'Oh—of course.' Holly got abruptly up from the wall, and then, realising the two men had not been introduced, she appended briefly, 'This is one of my colleagues, Stephen Brent. Steve—this is my father's assistant, Morgan Kane.'

'I guessed,' said Stephen distantly, making no attempt to shake hands, and Holly was loath to leave them with animosity fairly bristling between them.

As luck would have it, there was still a cup of coffee left in the jug when she charged back into the school kitchen. 'An unexpected visitor,' she explained to Hannah Dessai, who was washing her cup at the sink. 'I can't stop now. I'm afraid Steve will lose his temper.'

'Why? Who is it?' Hannah's dark eyes widened. 'Not your unwelcome house-guest?'

'Got it in one,' said Holly ruefully, scooping up the cup again and making for the door. Her lips twisted. 'I suppose my father asked him to check out *everything*.'

Outside again, she was relieved to see that so far the two men had not come to blows. On the contrary, as she drew nearer, she heard Morgan commenting on the beauty of the island, but Stephen's response was hardly complimentary.

'. . . yet you're prepared to deprive Miss Forsyth of its advantages, and dump her in some smelly London suburb,' he finished provokingly, and Holly caught her breath at this unwarranted attack.

'Steve,' she exclaimed, reaching them, but Morgan's voice overrode her anxious protest.

'I don't believe Hampstead deserves quite that description,' he observed mildly. 'And in any case, I'm only delivering Miss Forsyth's father's instructions. I don't have any influence, Mr Brent, one way or the other.'

'That's a bloody easy cop-out,' retorted Stephen angrily, his restraint suffering in the face of Morgan's calm indifference. 'I suppose you don't allow yourself to have an opinion. What are you? Some kind of yes-man, or something?'

'Or something,' agreed Morgan without rancour, making his way to the wall and lowering his weight on to it. Then, taking the coffee Holly proffered with a faintly sardonic smile, he added, 'Thanks. I never realised walking could take so much effort.'

'I expect you're not much used to exercise, are you,

Mr Kane?' Stephen waded into the attack again, and Holly sent him an imploring look. 'Too busy oiling palms and licking boots, I shouldn't wonder,' he appended unpleasantly. 'Don't you ever get sickened by doing someone else's dirty work?'

'Stephen, please!'

Holly was quite desperate, but Morgan was more than capable of handling himself, as she discovered. 'Someone has to keep the wheels of industry turning,' he remarked, his bland expression giving no hint of his real feelings. 'Dare I say, if we'd all—vegetated—on tropical islands all our lives, we'd still be running around in loin cloths and beating each other's brains out.' He paused. 'Or perhaps you would prefer that. You do have a decidedly primitive way of making your point, Mr Brent.'

'Why, you——'

'Stephen, for heaven's sake!' Holly stepped swiftly between them, facing the young West Indian with unconcealed impatience. 'You started this, remember? You can't blame Mo—Mr Kane for defending himself.'

'Well, what's he doing, coming here?' demanded Stephen, looking beyond her to where Morgan was drinking his coffee with cool composure. He glared at the older man resentfully. 'This is private property, Kane. You're not welcome here.'

Morgan finished the coffee in his cup and, setting it aside, rose somewhat cautiously to his feet. 'Very well,' he said, shifting his walking stick to his left hand and leaning on it heavily. 'I'll wait down on the quay. You won't object to giving me a lift home, will you, Holly? I told Harding I wouldn't need his assistance.'

Holly gazed at him frustratedly. 'You mean—you don't have any other means of getting back?'

'Well, I guess I could get a cab,' conceded Morgan drily. 'But I understood you finished at lunchtime.'

'I do.' Holly caught her lower lip tight between her teeth. 'But it's only eleven-thirty. I don't usually finish until two.'

'Ah.' Morgan absorbed this with a rueful grimace. 'I've evidently misunderstood what Lucinda told me.' He hesitated a moment, and then shrugged somewhat philosophically. 'No matter. I can wait.'

Holly glanced frustratedly at Stephen, and then, either unwilling, or unable, to endure the thought of Morgan dragging himself down to the quay, she intervened. 'You can't,' she exclaimed, aware of Stephen's disapproval but too conscious of Morgan's disability to pay it much heed. 'You can't walk down to the harbour, and you can't wait in the sun for two solid hours. You just can't?'

'Why not?' Once again, Stephen chose to intervene, his voice harsh and scathing. 'Heaven knows, the exercise will probably do him good.'

'Are you mad?'

Holly turned on him then, but it was Morgan who offered an alternative. 'What else can I do?' he enquired drily. 'Unless you choose to finish earlier than usual, of course.'

'Why should she?' Stephen swept aside the girl's protests and confronted the other man furiously. 'It's not her fault you fell off your horse! It's not her fault you haven't the skill to stay in a saddle! And it's certainly not her fault that the only horses you're used to are those you hang your clothes on!'

'Well, no one could say that of you,' responded Morgan mockingly, surveying Stephen's attire of short-sleeved shirt and wide-legged shorts with a distinctly malicious eye. 'As I said before—your style is decidedly neolithic, Mr Brent.'

Stephen's fists warned Holly of what he intended to do just a moment too late. Intent on keeping the two men apart, she had never considered the dangers to herself. Forcing her way between them, she didn't anticipate the blow until it hit her, and then the punch which should have connected with Morgan's jaw sent a stream of coloured lights exploding before her eyes.

She came round to find herself lying on the leather day-bed in the Reverend Frost's study. Hannah was seated beside her, applying a cooling sponge to her brow, while from somewhere close at hand, she could hear the low buzz of male voices.

'She's conscious, Mr Kane,' she heard Hannah say, as her eyelids flickered, and a moment later Morgan and the school principal came to look down at her.

'Thank God,' said Reverend Frost piously, and Morgan's lips twisted.

'Thank *you*, Miss Dessai,' he amended, and when the games mistress rose, he took her place. 'How are you feeling, Holly?' he added, running tentative fingers along the curve of her cheek. 'This is going to hurt like hell in the morning. Have you ever had a black eye before?'

'Not that I remember,' said Holly, finding it painful even to speak. Her head was aching and she felt a little sick. 'What happened? Did I pass out?'

'Not unreasonably, in the circumstances,' conceded Morgan drily. 'Still—it was one way of earning a couple of hours' remission, I suppose.' His lips twitched. 'Poor Brent. He thought he'd killed you.'

'It's no laughing matter, Mr Kane,' exclaimed Reverend Frost, intercepting Morgan's amusement. 'If what Stephen says is true, you were provoking him in the most insulting way possible. We don't criticise a man's appearance here. It's his worth as a human being we try to measure.'

'Oh, but——' began Holly, realising Morgan was not

about to say anything in his own defence, when he swiftly overrode her.

'Yes,' he said, glancing up at the headmaster, 'it was all my fault. Now, I suggest you allow me to take Miss Forsyth home. It's obvious she's not going to be able to continue with her lessons this morning.'

If the Reverend Frost wanted to protest, he refrained from doing so, restricting himself to a terse, 'Please drive carefully then.' For her part, Holly was immensely glad when someone lifted her off the couch to carry her to the buggy. She had closed her eyes against the wave of dizziness that had accompanied her attempt to remonstrate on Morgan's behalf, but she was horrified to discover that it was Morgan himself who was carrying her.

'I know,' he said, grunting a little as he descended the steps to the playground. 'I shouldn't be doing this. But Brent's disappeared and your scholarly principal didn't look strong enough, so what could I do?'

'You could have let me walk,' said Holly, though she swayed a little when he set her down beside the car. 'Thanks, anyway. But are you sure you're fit to drive?'

'Just give me the keys,' said Morgan flatly, though his skin had acquired a sheen of perspiration. 'It's amazing what anyone can do, if they have to. Now, get in, will you? Before your friend decides to finish what he started.'

Holly scrambled into the buggy. 'You're not afraid of Stephen, are you?'

'Afraid?' Morgan grimaced. 'Why not? He's quite a formidable character, isn't he?' He looked at her. 'Your boyfriend?'

'Stephen already has a wife,' said Holly crossly, expelling her breath in an upward motion. She sighed. 'I don't believe you're afraid of Stephen. Where is he? Where did he go?'

'Let's not stop to find out,' said Morgan, levering his length behind the wheel and wincing as his spine protested. 'Okay,' he stifled a painful groan, 'just tell me how to get back to your house. I, for one, could do with something stronger than coffee.'

Lucinda was horrified when she saw Holly's face, and Holly, who had only had a glimpse of herself in the wing-mirror of the buggy, hastened into the hall, where there was a mirror.

'My God!' she was whispering, as Morgan appeared behind her, and for once she was indifferent to the sallowness of his skin.

'It will fade,' he remarked tautly, as she brushed her fingers over the curve of her cheekbone where the swelling began. 'It's an advantage really. You can always tell your father I did it.'

Holly gasped and turned to face him. 'I wouldn't do that.'

'Why not?'

'Because I wouldn't. I don't tell lies, Mr Kane.'

'Not even to your boyfriend?'

'I don't have a boyfriend.'

'All right. Stephen what's-his-name, then,' said Morgan wearily, beginning to drag himself in the direction of her father's study. 'You told him I was— nice, apparently. But you don't believe that.' He paused in the open doorway, and gave her a penetrating look. 'And you're right. I'm not nice, Miss Forsyth; I'm decidedly nasty. And what's more, I've decided that we're leaving tomorrow, not three days from now. I've had enough of desert-island living. Give me the old concrete jungle every time!'

CHAPTER EIGHT

HOLLY came down for dinner with much reluctance. She hated the idea of having to expose her bruised face to the other members of her father's household, and while careful make-up had disguised most of her skin's discolouration, it could not erase the ugly swelling that gave her features a slightly one-sided appearance. But her father had specifically asked that she should join him for dinner and, as she had no wish to re-kindle their animosity towards one another, she had agreed. So far, they were maintaining a rather precarious truce, and although Holly's resentment had not dissipated, other considerations had tended to overshadow the bitterness she still felt towards Andrew Forsyth.

Not least of these was her own unwilling attraction towards Morgan Kane. It was irrational, and obviously not reciprocated, but it was there, just the same; a powerful, and uncontrollable, force that subsequent events had only strengthened, not diminished.

It was incredible to think it was only ten days since she had imagined she might effect *his* downfall. When her father's telegram had arrived, she had anticipated Morgan's appearance with grim purpose. Two years had caused her to believe—quite wrongly as it turned out—that the youthful feelings she had nurtured for her father's personal assistant had long deserted her. And even when she saw him again, she had continued to compound the fallacy. It wasn't until their confrontation, among the burnt-out cabins at the plantation, that she had conceived her mistake, and when Morgan had kissed her, her worst fears were realised.

Of course, she had fought the weakness, understanding only too well what it could mean. She was not a child any longer to dismiss such feelings as a form of hero-worship. She had admired Morgan as a child, but she admired him as a woman now, even though he had given her little encouragement. Oh, he had wanted her, physically at least, on more than one occasion. But he was a man, after all, who was no doubt used to female company. And ten days was a long time, when he had had little else to think about. The fact that he had been able to control his baser instincts proved that his was not an all-consuming passion. No doubt, now that he was back in London again, he would resume his faintly patronising attitude towards her, and no doubt that was just as well.

Nevertheless, she had known a totally unworthy sense of achievement the morning they left the island, when Lucinda admitted that Stephen had been admitted to the local hospital the previous evening.

'Micah heard the poor man had a couple of cracked ribs,' she declared, watching Holly closely. 'I suppose you wouldn't know nothing about that.'

'*I* don't,' Holly replied honestly. 'Perhaps that's something you should speak to *Mr* Morgan about.'

Lucinda hadn't, of course. And Morgan himself had not mentioned the affair again. But for a while, Holly had nurtured the idea that perhaps Morgan did care for her, after all. A notion which had been swiftly obliterated by his coolness to her since.

Now, with one hand raised to protect her cheek, Holly entered the library of her father's house. An elegant, book-lined room, it accommodated Andrew Forsyth's famous collection of first editions, safely protected behind burglar-proof glass doors. But it was also a comfortable room and one where her father's guests normally gathered to have drinks before the more formal business of the evening began. Not that Holly expected any guests this evening. Her father had assured her there would be just the two of them, and she was relying on that.

It was an unpleasant surprise, therefore, to find she had been mistaken. Instead of finding her father in the library, waiting for her, she found a woman there; a slim, attractive, dark-haired woman, helping herself to ice from a silver-plated bucket. She turned as Holly entered the room, and the girl was not unaware of the swift, but comprehensive, appraisal she was given before the woman's eyes returned to her face. Then, with a smile lifting her lips but not quite reaching her eyes, the woman came towards her, holding out her hand as if she, not Holly, belonged there. Holly felt there was something familiar about her, but she couldn't think what. No doubt she was someone she had seen here in the past. But, as Holly had seldom attended her father's dinner parties, she had known few of his staff or their wives outside the office.

'How lovely to see you again, Holly,' the woman was saying now, and the girl thought how typical it was of her father to do this to her. She was almost tempted to turn round and go back to her own room, except that she had no absolute guarantee that he would not send someone after her. 'Does your eye hurt? Morgan told me what happened. Such a silly accident, and just when you were coming home.'

Morgan? Holly blinked. The woman must be someone from the office then. Morgan's secretary, perhaps. Or her father's. Though, she pondered, did secretaries wear Christian Dior dresses or move in a cloud of what Holly was able to recognise as Gucci perfume?

'You don't remember me, do you?' the woman added, close enough now for Holly to see the faint lines of dissipation around her mouth. 'But I remember you. Even without that bruise, which does single you out, I will admit.'

Holly caught her lower lip between her teeth. 'I'm sorry,' she said, aware of the stiffness of her voice, but unable to do anything about it. She was relieved she had not come down to dinner in the sweater and jeans she had been wearing all day. She might easily have done so, even though she knew her father liked to change in the evenings. May in London was so much cooler than May in the Caribbean, and she had known that wearing a thin silk or jersey dress would have left her shivering. Instead, she had compromised, dressing in a wide-sleeved fine wool jump-suit, with a flattering cowl neckline and trousers that ended just above her ankle. It was black, and she had hoped its darkness would help to disguise her injuries. Even with her father, she was intensely conscious of the disfigurement, and now she welcomed her foresight. This woman had no qualms about drawing attention to the defect, and Holly wondered again who she could be to be so insensitive. The woman was older than she had at first imagined. Not one of her father's dolly-birds, she was prepared to bet. Yet, it was possible that Andrew Forsyth's tastes had changed in her absence, and her lips tightened involuntarily at this possible explanation.

Now, holding up her head, she faced her adversary with grim determination. 'Do you work for my father, Miss—Mrs——?' she enquired politely, and was rewarded by a gurgle of amusement.

'Heavens, no,' the female responded swiftly. 'But my—my ex-husband does.' She paused. 'I'm Alison Kane. Your father and I were able to help one another while Morgan was away, and he suggested it might be a good idea if you and I became friends.'

Holly felt her jaw beginning to drop and rectified the

fault. 'M—Mrs Kane,' she murmured, moistening her lips. 'Of course.' She should have studied the woman more closely. Although she had never actually been introduced to Morgan's wife, she did remember seeing them together at one of her father's dinners some time ago. Some *years* ago, she corrected herself drily. It had to be at least five.

'I knew you'd remember,' Alison remarked now, swirling the ice in her glass with an idle finger and then raising the same finger to her lips. Her lips twisted. 'I hope Morgan didn't give you a hard time.'

Holly drew a breath. 'Morgan?'

'Your father told me you weren't keen to come back to London,' she explained carelessly. 'I'm surprised. I'd have thought London held more for a girl of your age than an island in the Caribbean.'

'Would you?' Holly was finding it incredibly difficult to be civil to the woman, and her mind was a chaotic turmoil of half-formed thoughts and wild exaggerations. What was Alison Kane doing here? Why did her father desire them to be friends? And did Morgan know that his employer and his ex-wife had become so intimate?

'Oh, I'm sure everyone would envy you a few weeks in the sun,' Alison was continuing, 'but two years! I mean—weren't you bored silly?'

'I paint,' said Holly, pulling herself together and moving across the room to help herself to a Bacardi and Coke. It was a mixture she had come to enjoy during her time in the West Indies and, although she seldom imbibed very freely, tonight she felt in need of a stiffening drink.

'Oh, yes.' Alison turned to watch her. 'Andrew told me.' *Andrew?* 'But surely that didn't occupy all your time.'

'I taught,' conceded Holly unwillingly, swallowing a generous portion of her drink. 'At the school on the island.' She raised her glass in a self-mocking salute. 'One of the advantages of an expensive education.'

'Even so,' Alison considered, 'one wonders why a girl with your—undoubted advantages, should choose such an existence.'

'Didn't my father tell you that, too?' enquired Holly, a definite edge to her voice now, and Alison looked distinctly relieved when the man himself came strolling into the room to join them.

Holly's tongue clove to her upper lip as her father put a hand on the woman's shoulder in passing, before continuing on to where his daughter was standing. 'I see you and Alison have been renewing your acquaintance,' he remarked evenly, regarding Holly with guarded sympathy, and she thought how typical it was that he should underplay his involvement.

'Mrs—Mrs Kane and I have never met—before tonight, that is,' she responded tautly, suffering his kiss on her unbruised cheek. 'She says you and she have—been of some use to one another while—while your assistant was away.'

'Morgan?' Andrew arched his rather bushy brows, and pulled a wry face. 'Well, yes. I suppose you could say that.' He cast an acknowledging smile in Alison's direction. 'But first—tell me how you feel this evening, my dear? You still look a little pale.'

'I'm fine.'

Holly didn't want his sympathy, not now, not while Alison Kane was looking on with that decidedly condescending air. What was she doing here? What was her father up to now? And why couldn't she hate him, when he evidently found her so easy to manipulate?

'Well ...' Andrew smiled now, apparently prepared to overlook her ungraciousness. 'Let me say, it is good to have you back again. I've missed you, and— well——'

'... you never thought you would,' put in Holly tightly, wishing he would revert to the unfeeling monster she remembered. She paused, and then added provokingly, 'I thought we were dining alone. I must have misunderstood.'

Andrew's expression mirrored his impatience for only a moment, and then urbanity re-asserted itself. It was obvious he was determined to appear before Alison Kane in the role of the all-forgiving father, and Holly wondered bitterly if he was acting this way because of the twins. Maybe he wanted her to think he was a good parent. Or had he another motive for trying to win his daughter's approval?

'I thought you wouldn't mind if Alison joined us,' he responded now, lifting the decanter of Scotch and pouring a generous measure into a glass. 'Can I freshen your drink? What is it? Coca Cola?'

'Bacardi and Coke, actually,' said Holly, extending the glass for his attention. It crossed her mind that, if she drank enough of the raw spirit, she might succeed in numbing her brain as well as her senses.

'Well, you see, I had to call on Alison's help a few days ago,' her father explained now. 'I had this Arab delegation to entertain, and you know how important it is to have a hostess on those occasions. After I received your telex, I didn't know what I was going to do, but a call from Alison solved my problem.'

'A call?' Holly thought she was probably being very obtuse, but her father seemed more than willing to elucidate.

'Alison was trying to get in touch with Morgan. When she couldn't, she called me.' He smiled at the other woman. 'A fortunate occurrence for both of us.'

'I see.'

Holly was trying very hard not to show the feelings of pain and confusion that were gripping her. What was going on here? she asked herself unsteadily. Was she to take her father's words at their face value? Had Alison's intervention merely served a useful purpose? Or was this his way of telling her that her services were no longer required?

The entrance of a fourth member of the group brought her head round with a start. But the man who had followed her father into the room was instantly recognisable. In a dark, three-piece suit and a pale grey shirt and tie, Morgan Kane was unnervingly familiar, his narrowed gaze flicking carelessly over herself and his ex-wife before coming to rest on his employer's square face.

'Sorry I'm late,' Morgan remarked, apparently not surprised to find Alison present. 'It took some time to get through to San Francisco, but I've spoken to Fleming and he's handling the contracts himself.'

'If you're sure.' Andrew shook his head. 'Oh well, what will you have to drink? Scotch?'

'Sounds good.' Morgan inclined his head. Then, with studied charm, he greeted the two women, 'Alison.' He inclined his head. 'And Holly. How do you feel this evening?'

Holly wondered what he would say if she told him the truth—that she was anxious and bewildered, and not at all informed as to what was going on here. Even his arrival had not followed any pattern she might have anticipated. Didn't he mind that his ex-wife was his employer's guest? Had he known in advance that she and Andrew had become better acquainted?

Her confusion left a space which Alison very competently filled. 'I think Holly is bearing up very well, don't you?' she remarked, giving the girl a decidedly patronising smile. 'Poor child! I'm sure she wishes you'd never gone out to the island. I mean— what did you say to provoke this man so? You really should watch your tongue, Morgan. Particularly when someone else can be hurt.'

'I'm afraid *I* don't have that faculty,' responded Morgan smoothly, and Holly was amazed to see his ex-wife's face redden now. 'And she isn't a child, Alison. If she were, her father wouldn't have sent for her.'

Holly expected her father to intervene then, and he did; though once again not in the way she had anticipated. 'Isn't this conversation getting a bit intense, Morgan?' he protested persuasively. 'Holly knows this is her home and she's always welcome here. Hell,' he grunted, 'it wasn't my idea to send her off to the Caribbean.'

Morgan shrugged, accepting the drink Andrew held out to him and swallowing half of it at a gulp. 'I guess we've all done things we're not proud of,' he remarked, his gaze lingering longest on Holly's flushed face. 'You never did tell me how you're feeling? Or do you need notice of that question?'

'I'm—much better,' said Holly steadily, still amazed by his defence of her earlier. 'How—how about you?'

Morgan shrugged. 'I get a twinge now and again, and I was pretty stiff after the flight, but otherwise I'm okay.' He grimaced. 'You know how it is. When you're busy, you don't have time to think about yourself. And—subsequent events have kind of got in the way.'

'You sound as if you object to the fact that Andrew and I have become friends,' put in Alison sharply, apparently recovered from her momentary lapse. 'He said you wouldn't, but I wasn't so sure.'

'Object?' Morgan's short laugh was almost insulting. 'Why should I object?' and Holly could see Alison's eyes sparkling at his deliberately humorous way of responding. 'Honestly, Allie, you have my blessing.' His eyes shifted mockingly to his employer. 'As a matter of fact, I'm sure you have a lot in common.'

In the few silent moments that followed Morgan's announcement, Holly could fairly feel the hostility emanating from the other woman, but then Andrew took Alison's arm. 'Let me get you another drink, my dear,' he said, successfully drawing her attention away from her ex-husband, and in the hiatus that followed, Holly and Morgan were able to speak without fear of interruption.

'He didn't warn you, did he?' Morgan observed quietly, watching her face. 'Your father,' he added. 'He didn't tell you that he and Alison have been seeing one another?'

Holly permitted herself one brief glance in her father's direction, and then shook her head. 'No.' She frowned. 'What is there to tell?'

'Did he say anything?'

'Not until this evening.' Holly tried to think. 'Before you came, he explained how—how Alison had helped him to entertain some Arab delegation.'

Morgan nodded. 'I see.'

Holly gazed at him blankly. 'What are you implying?'

Morgan studied the liquid in his glass. 'I'm not—implying anything.'

'Is there something else I should know?'

Morgan's mouth twisted. 'Maybe. Maybe not.'

Holly sighed. 'Has—has my father discussed it with you?'

'His relationship with Alison? Not exactly.'

'Then——'

'Alison couldn't wait to tell me herself.'

Holly hesitated. 'Do—do you see her often?' Her heart constricted at the thought.

'No.' Morgan's response was laconic. 'But we do speak on the telephone from time to time.'

'Oh.' Holly nodded.

'Just because we're divorced, doesn't mean we don't

have certain commitments to one another,' he explained quietly. 'We have children.'

Holly swallowed. 'Your sons.'

'My sons,' he agreed levelly.

'They—they live with your—with Alison?'

'At present.'

Holly's tongue circled her lips. 'Are you hoping to change that?'

Morgan grimaced. 'There's always hope.'

'Your—Alison has custody?'

'For the time being,' he conceded. 'Do you want another drink?'

Holly shook her head, moving after him nevertheless. 'About—about this business with—with Alison and my father: don't you really mind?'

'No. I don't really mind,' he assured her drily. 'Do you?'

Holly made a confused gesture. 'I don't understand what's going on.'

'It's quite simple.' Morgan tasted the drink he had poured himself and, apparently satisfied with its flavour, transferred his attention back to her. 'While I was—incapacitated, shall we say?—Alison approached your father for a loan.' He pulled a wry face. 'I should explain. My ex-wife lives to the limit of her income, and my prolonged absence delayed a cheque that was due to her.'

Holly's eyes widened. 'I see.'

'Do you?' Morgan regarded her steadily. 'I wonder.'

'My father has had four wives already,' she murmured, glancing half apprehensively over her shoulder. 'But surely——'

'Indeed.' Morgan seemed to tire of the discussion, and swiftly swallowed the remainder of his Scotch. 'Time will tell,' he appended, allowing his glass to slide back on to the tray with a definite thud. 'Here's Mrs Percy. Dinner must be ready.'

Holly followed the housekeeper's broad figure into the dining room with some regret. Mrs Percy's arrival to announce that the meal was waiting had successfully terminated her conversation with Morgan, and she doubted her ability to achieve such an intimacy with him again this evening. A glance at his dark face had elicited a definite withdrawal on his part, and she wondered if he was already regretting being so frank with her.

The dining room overlooked the floodlit terrace at the back of the house, and candles were the only illumination necessary. It was not yet dark outside, but it had been a dull day and the flickering light was welcome. It enhanced the beauty of shining silver cutlery and fine bone china, reflecting itself over and over in the long-stemmed crystal glasses. A centrepiece of pale cream roses surrounding a scarlet orchid was appealing, and monogrammed napkin rings glinted at every place.

Because the table was rectangular in shape and capable of accommodating at least five times their number, only one end of its polished surface was in use. Retrieving his role as host, Andrew directed them to their appointed positions, ensuring that Holly and Alison faced one another on his right and left respectively, with Morgan occupying the chair furthest away from him, on the same side as his daughter. It looked like a deliberate attempt to point up the fact of Morgan's separation from his wife, and although Alison was evidently flattered by Andrew's obvious preference, nevertheless, her attitude was less than friendly towards the other two people present.

The first course was a chilled consommé, and although Holly wasn't particularly hungry, she made a determined effort to appear as if she was enjoying it. But she was intensely conscious of Alison's less than cordial appraisal, and she wondered with a momentary sense of panic what she would do if the other woman did marry her father. She had not always liked her previous stepmothers, but she had never actually *dis*liked them either. She had simply tried to keep out of their way. Somehow, she knew, with Alison it would be different. Not least, because Holly's own feelings were involved.

'So——' As if realising that the undercurrents he could feel were not about to disperse by themselves, Andrew laid down his spoon and rested his elbows on the table. 'This is an auspicious occasion. My daughter is sitting at my table again after an absence of almost two years, and Morgan—it's good to have you back. The Forsyth Corporation doesn't run half so smoothly without you at the helm.'

Morgan shifted in his chair, his lean thigh brushing Holly's as he did so. 'Thank you for the compliment,' he conceded, though his tone was faintly sardonic. 'However, I'm sure you'd manage perfectly well without me, Andrew. No one is indispensable.'

'You are.' The older man's eyes challenged him. 'There is no one else in the whole of the company who knows more about my business than you do.'

Morgan inclined his head. 'If you say so.'

'I do say so.' Andrew picked up his spoon again and took a mouthful of his soup. 'And I think you know how important to me you are, whatever our private differences.'

Morgan made no response, and Holly permitted herself a sidelong glance in his direction. Now what? she wondered uneasily. Were there other considerations here, other influences she was still unaware of? And if so, how did they affect Morgan?

The reappearance of Mrs Percy to clear their plates gave all of them a temporary respite, and by the time

Andrew had carved the rib of beef that followed any response Morgan might have made had been successfully avoided. Instead, Alison made some trite comment about the food, and Andrew expanded the discussion to include the rather fine wine he was offering with the meal.

For her part, Holly was glad not to be included in the conversation. It gave her the opportunity to reconsider everything Morgan had said, both here and in the library. It was curious, she thought, how swiftly circumstances could change. One incident—or in this case an *accident*—had altered the whole course of their lives. If it had never happened, she and Morgan would have returned to London, and the feelings she had tried so hard to control would have been stifled at birth. In addition to which, Alison would not have become involved with her father, and this present situation would not now be taking place.

'You didn't tell me what you thought of the island,' Andrew commented suddenly, looking at the younger man. 'And the house: it was quite a show place once.'

Morgan allowed himself a moment's grace, and then said evenly, 'The island's beautiful, but the house needs some renovation. If it's allowed to deteriorate any further, some of the wood will be beyond redemption.'

'Is that so?' As Holly reluctantly acknowledged Morgan's unemotional assessment, her father gave it further thought. 'You didn't tell me this, Holly. At no time do I recall you asking for money for the property.'

'No, Father.' Holly was involved, whether she liked it or not, and she drew a steadying breath. 'I didn't think you'd be interested. After all, you don't like the island.'

'Oh, I wouldn't say that.' Andrew gave Alison a conspiratorial look. 'It's the ideal place, if you want to get away from it all. Shady palms, soft beaches—and the most delightful water in the whole of the Caribbean.'

'It sounds wonderful,' murmured Alison predictably, and Holly's hands balled into fists in her lap. 'I've never been to the West Indies, actually.' Her eyes turned to her ex-husband, and Holly could see the malice gleaming in their depths. 'Morgan was always too busy to take me.'

'I wonder whose fault that was,' Holly exclaimed recklessly, stung as much by her father's hypocrisy as Alison's affectation, and Andrew pulled a wry face.

'Touché,' he remarked, giving his daughter a grudging commendation. 'It seems your trip to the Caribbean had sharpened your wit, my dear. Whatever happened to the rebellious teenager I remember?'

'She grew up,' said Holly, forcing back the hot tide of colour that threatened to betray her. 'It was bound to happen sooner or later, Father. I'm sorry if you're disappointed.'

'I didn't say that.' Andrew was unwillingly defensive, and his tone had an edge to it when he turned back to his assistant. 'Are you in any way responsible for my daughter's emotional outburst, Morgan? I can't believe she's changed so much, all by herself.'

'You flatter me.'

Although Holly was discomfited, Morgan was unperturbed, and it was left to Alison to say irritably, 'It's true. Morgan doesn't have any emotions, do you, *darling*? He's never done anything reckless in his entire life!'

Even Andrew looked a little taken aback by the vehemency of Alison's statement, and in an effort to show he had not taken her words seriously, he smiled. 'Perhaps we should ask Holly if she agrees with you,' he declared, pouring himself more wine. 'Well, my dear, do you think Morgan's as cold-blooded as Alison would have us believe?'

Holly hesitated, and then, meeting the older woman's

gaze she decided she had nothing to lose. 'No more than you are, Father,' she responded, keeping her tone purposefully light. 'When you know my father better, Mrs Kane, you'll realise he likes to be provocative. It makes for interesting dinner conversation, don't you think?'

The woman's eyes spat malevolence across the table, but Holly refused to be intimidated by it. Besides, if Alison believed her father was some love-sick youth, who could be manipulated at will, she ought to be made aware of it. Andrew Forsyth seldom did anything unless it was to further his own ends, and if he was seriously considering a fifth marriage, Alison should know what she was letting herself in for.

'You didn't have to defend me, you know,' Morgan remarked later, under cover of Mrs Percy collecting the dinner plates. His mouth tilted mockingly. 'You should have agreed with her.'

'Why?' Holly took a breath and faced him. 'It wouldn't be true.'

'Wouldn't it?' Morgan cast a warning look at his ex-wife, who was evidently trying to hear what they were saying, but without any success.

'No.' Holly bent her head. 'You have emotions. You're just afraid to display them, that's all.'

Morgan uttered a low oath. 'Oh, really!'

'Yes, really.' Holly lifted her shoulders. 'I wish you'd stop behaving as if I was some irresponsible child. I'm not a child. I know what I want.'

Morgan's mouth compressed. 'This isn't the place to have a discussion of this kind,' he retorted harshly. But realising no one could see her, Holly spread her fingers on his thigh.

'What alternative do I have?' she countered, feeling the muscles tense beneath her hand. 'When can we see one another alone?'

'We can't.' With a determined effort, Morgan removed her fingers, and gave her a threatening look. 'Don't,' he added, returning her hand to her lap, and Holly felt the frustration of knowing that so far as he was concerned they were as far apart as ever.

It was a relief when the meal was over, and she could escape to the comparative privacy of the library. At least there she did not have to combat Alison's malicious gaze and, as soon as the coffee had been served, she was hoping to make her excuses and return to her room.

But, to her dismay, Alison installed herself in the armchair beside her and, as Andrew had detained Morgan at the table, briefly she was at the older woman's mercy.

'Tell me,' Alison said confidingly, though her expression was far from friendly, 'did you know that Morgan is leaving Forsyth's?'

'Leaving?' Holly could not prevent the dismay she was feeling from colouring the word, and Alison looked pleased.

'Yes, leaving,' she declared spitefully. 'He told Andrew of his decision when he got back from the Caribbean two days ago. Didn't he discuss it with you?'

'No.' Holly made an effort to conceal how the news had affected her and shook her head. 'I—why would he?'

Alison's eyes narrowed. 'Oh, I don't know. Perhaps because he must know how you'd take the news.' She shrugged. 'He does know you're in love with him, doesn't he? Oh, of course, he must do. He may be a machine, but he's not unperceptive.'

Holly caught her breath. 'I think you're imagining things, Mrs Kane——'

'Am I?' Alison lay back in her chair, evidently satisfied that she had succeeded in her objective. 'Is that why you're looking so sick all of a sudden? Because I've made a mistake? I don't think so.'

Holly licked her lips. 'Are you saying that—that's why he's——'

'. . . leaving Forsyth's?' Alison's laughter was cruel. 'Heavens, no! Can't you think of a better reason than that?'

Holly gazed at her. 'Because—because of—of you and my father?'

'What else?' Alison made a careless gesture. 'Morgan may not have been the most ardent lover, but he wanted me. He fought the divorce, you know. He never wanted us to split up. So you can imagine how he feels now that Andrew and I are such close friends!'

CHAPTER NINE

MORGAN awakened the next morning with a thumping head and a mouth that tasted like a sewer. Rolling over to consult the clock on his bedside table, he saw the reason for his state of health. The whisky bottle he had emptied the night before resided sordidly beside the empty tumbler, and he grimaced at the memory of how it came to be there.

How Alison would like to see him now, he reflected sourly, pushing back his hair and staring blearily at the clock. *God!* it was half past nine already! She might not like the connotations of his hangover, but she would surely revel in his misery.

Pushing back the quilt, he swung his legs out of bed, wincing at the stabbing pain this elicited in his temple. He had been a fool to indulge himself so freely. Nothing was worth this sacrifice, though he had not thought so when he went to bed.

Turning on the tap in the shower, he stepped beneath the chilling spray, feeling every single droplet like needles on his skin. Fragile, he reflected savagely; that was how he felt. As weak and as vulnerable as a bloody open wound!

And why? he asked himself impatiently. Because he was attracted to a girl half his age! Because, for the first time in his life, he had found something—*someone*—beside whom his work, his *ambition*, faded in significance.

It was stupid, and he had fought the overwhelming needs she aroused inside him; but sooner or later those needs were going to prove irresistible, and when that time came, he intended to be far away

144

from London—and Holly.

He had been offered a job in the United States. A Boston firm, specialising in electronics, needed a company secretary, and Morgan was already considering their proposal. In the past, it had been an occupational hazard, coping with firms which, knowing of his success with Forsyth's, had attempted to lure him away with tempting propositions. But this was the first time Morgan had actually given such a proposition serious consideration. It had crossed his mind that the more lucrative salary he was being offered would enable him to buy a house in Boston, thus providing a home for Jeff and Jon. The idea of getting his sons far away from Alison's clutches was appealing, too, and if she was hoping to marry Andrew, this might be a good time to press for shared custody.

He felt a little more human when he emerged from the shower. The stimulation had eventually proved beneficial, and although he swallowed a couple of aspirins with a glass of water instead of his usual morning cup of coffee, he saw to his relief that his hand was quite steady on the razor.

The young woman who occupied the flat next door arrived just as Morgan was knotting his tie. The mother of two school-age infants, she supplemented her husband's income as a taxi driver by cleaning Morgan's flat as well as her own, an arrangement which suited both of them very well.

'You're late, aren't you?' she asked, letting herself in with the key Morgan had given her, and then looking somewhat embarrassed at finding him still at home. 'I'm sorry. I thought I heard you go out over an hour ago. Do you want me to come back later?'

'No, that's okay.' Morgan heaved a sigh as he slid his arms into the jacket of his suit. 'I'm leaving right now. I'm afraid this place is in quite a mess. I overslept.'

'That's all right.' The young woman smiled. 'I've got nothing else to do today.' She paused. 'Would you like me to make you a casserole, too?'

'You spoil me,' said Morgan gallantly, though right then the idea of a casserole made him feel slightly nauseous. Nevertheless, he thanked her warmly, and she thought that, when Mr Kane smiled, almost any woman would promise him anything.

Even though the rush hour was over, the London streets were still teeming with traffic, the tourists taking over where the commuters left off. Morgan, who invariably used the underground to get to work, had recklessly taken a taxi this morning, and it was after eleven by the time he entered the imposing offices of the Forsyth Corporation.

'I bet you wish you were still in the Caribbean, Mr Kane,' commented Ben Harris, the commissionaire, nodding at the overcast skies that threatened rain later. 'Still, maybe not,' he amended, awkwardly. 'How is your back this morning?'

'Well, I'm still standing,' remarked Morgan drily, giving him a sympathetic grin. 'Don't worry about it. I shan't need a wheelchair for some time yet—I hope.'

'That you won't,' declared Ben fervently, grateful for the reprieve. 'You take it easy, Mr Kane.'

'Thanks.'

Morgan gave him a half-mocking salute as he stepped into the lift, and then, as the metal box bore him upward, he turned his attention to less personal matters.

His secretary, Teresa Michaels, was taking a coffee break when he entered his suite of offices. She had evidently decided he would not be putting in an appearance that morning, and she was deep in the pages of a magazine.

'Oh—Mr Kane!' she exclaimed, putting the magazine

aside and getting up, all in one motion, almost overbalancing her coffee in the process. 'I—you're late!'

'I know.' Morgan rescued the coffee and set the cup more securely on her desk. 'But before I do anything, I'd like some of this myself.'

'Of course.' Teresa hurried across the room to where a perspex jug percolated on a low heat. Taking a cup and saucer from the cabinet below, she poured the coffee, added two spoons of brown sugar and carried it back to him. 'There you are. Black, as you like it.'

'Sweetened, but not stirred,' remarked Morgan wryly, raising the cup to his lips. 'Hmm, that tastes good.' He savoured the aromatic liquid. 'So—is there anything urgent wanting my attention?'

'Just Mr Forsyth,' said Teresa, picking up the mail she had sorted earlier. 'There are one or two letters that need your personal attention.' She flicked over the envelopes and handed him one. 'That's from Goldman's, if you remember. They were in touch before you went away. I think they're afraid the delay might mean Forsyth's are having second thoughts about the deal.' She frowned. 'The rest aren't that important. I've drafted replies to those I could, and the others can be dealt with later.'

Morgan took the letters and smiled. 'What would I do without you?' he essayed, making his way across the office to the door that led into his own sanctum. Then he paused and looked at her. 'What did Mr Forsyth want? Did he say?'

'No.' Teresa shook her head. 'But he's phoned at least three times in the last hour. Didn't he know you were going to be late?'

'I didn't know myself until I woke up,' responded Morgan drily. 'Okay, Teresa; get him for me, will you? But if he's not available, get me Henry Goldman instead.'

'Yes, Mr Kane.'

Teresa resumed her seat at her desk and Morgan closed his office door behind him. Then, taking his coffee with him, he walked to the long windows which overlooked London's busy streets far below. He would miss this view, he reflected sombrely. No doubt his office in Boston would be equally luxurious, but he would miss the friends and acquaintances he had built up over twenty years at Forsyth's. It would be lonely, too; at least, initially. He knew few people in Boston, and those he did know were married, with wives and families of their own. But he *had* a family, he reminded himself severely. And it was time he made a stand for the right to have a say in their future.

The telephone on his desk gave off its subdued buzz and, abandoning his stance by the window, Morgan came to answer it. 'Mr Forsyth for you, Mr Kane,' said Teresa, when he lifted the receiver, and he heard the distinctive click as she put his employer on the line.

'Morgan!' Andrew's voice was harsh and accusing. 'Where the devil have you been?'

Morgan sank down into the leather chair behind his desk. 'I slept in,' he replied laconically. 'I didn't realise there was anything spoiling. What is it? An unscheduled board meeting? Or has Harry Goldman been crying in your ear?'

Andrew expelled his breath noisily. 'You slept in!' he echoed, ignoring the rest of what Morgan had said. 'My God!' There was a trace of humour in his voice now. 'And I thought you must be having an early morning meeting with Shafer's.'

Morgan caught his lower lip between his teeth. 'I wouldn't do that, Andrew. Not on your time. If I do choose to accept Lewis Shafer's offer, I'll do it when you're not paying me.'

'Dammit, Morgan!' Andrew sounded frustrated now. 'You're not seriously thinking of leaving us. I won't let you do this. I can't!

'Andrew——'

'No, dammit, I won't talk about this over the phone. You get yourself in here. Before I blow a gasket!'

'Andrew, I've got work——'

'And I'm the boss!' retorted the older man aggressively. And then, as if realising his blustering would get him nowhere with Morgan, he added wheedlingly, 'Humour, me, boy. Please.'

Morgan shook his head. 'All right. All right.' He took a breath. 'Give me five minutes.'

When he entered Andrew's office a few minutes later, he found his employer impatiently pacing the rug before his desk. With his head bent forward and his hands clasped behind his back, he resembled a rather irate grizzly, and the younger man was not unaware of the prestige it had cost him to make his appeal.

'Well, and not before time,' he exclaimed, when Morgan appeared. 'Sit down. Sit down.' He gestured to the comfortable chair that faced his desk. 'Shall I ask Maggie to bring us some coffee?'

'No thanks. Not for me. I've just had some,' said Morgan, lowering his lean frame into the chair. 'But if you want——'

'I don't.' Andrew circled his desk to face the other man. 'Dammit, Morgan, we're speaking to one another like strangers. I want to know what's happened to make you feel this way.'

'I thought I explained——'

'Well, you didn't.' Andrew dropped down into his own chair and rested his arms upon the desk. 'Look—I don't know what Shafer's have offered you but, whatever it is, I'll meet it. Better than that, I'll give you five per cent more. I can't say fairer than that, can I?'

'No.' Morgan inclined his head. 'But, I told you: it's not the money. I just feel it's time for a change——'

'Bullshit!' Andrew uttered an oath. 'I don't believe that, and you wouldn't expect me to. It's Alison, isn't it? Oh, don't bother to deny it, I know. You had no intention of working in America until you learned she and I had been seeing one another. Isn't that the truth?'

'No. 'Morgan sighed. 'Andrew, think! I didn't even know you'd seen Alison until after I'd told you what I was considering.'

Andrew groaned. 'But it doesn't make sense! You and I have always worked well together. Hell, isn't that why I promoted you over the heads of Parsons and that crowd? I stuck my neck out for you, Morgan, and this is how you repay me.'

Morgan shook his head. 'I'm sorry.'

'Sorry's not good enough.'

'What more can I say?' Morgan lifted his shoulders.

'You can tell Shafer to go——'

Andrew's suggestion was rather colourful, and Morgan pulled a wry face. 'Somehow I don't think I will.'

'Why not?' Andrew slammed his palms down on to the leather surface of his desk. 'I don't get this, Morgan. Before you went away there wasn't a hint that you might be looking for an alternative position. Now, suddenly, you want a change of scene.' His jaw compressed. 'You know, if I didn't know you so well, I might be tempted to wonder if Holly hasn't played some part in your decision.'

'You're crazy!' Morgan managed to keep his tone light. 'How could your daughter be involved?'

'I don't know.' Andrew grunted. 'She's not a bad-looking wench. Less like her mother now, you know. Since she lost that frail, waif-like air. Ought to get the boys buzzing about like bees round a honey-pot. Once she loses that bruise on her cheek, of course. Rather unfortunate, that. How did you say it happened?'

'I told you, Andrew. It was an accident——'

'Yes. Some chap who wanted to sock you on the jaw, eh?'

'That's right.'

'And why was that?'

'You *know*, Andrew. We had a—difference of opinion.'

'Over Holly?'

'No.' Morgan kept his tone level with difficulty. 'The fellow just took a dislike to me, I guess. He—he resented the fact that Holly was being forced to leave the island.'

'Forced?' Andrew snorted. 'For heaven's sake, I did the girl a favour! Wasting her youth out there. I bet she's glad to be back now she's here.'

Morgan made no response to this, and Andrew regarded him with growing irritation. 'So, is that it?' he demanded, and the younger man frowned.

'Is what it?'

Andrew sighed. 'Is Holly the reason you want to leave?'

'No. I've told you——'

'I know what you've said.' Andrew hunched his shoulders. 'But people don't walk out of positions of authority just because they fancy a change.'

Morgan's teeth ground together. 'So what's your solution?'

Andrew shook his head. 'Hell, I don't know. I'm tired of trying to find an answer. As I say, if it's not Alison—and I'm not absolutely convinced of that, mind you—it must be something to do with Holly.' He paused, and then smote his hand on to the desk again. 'I've got it! It's because she didn't want to come back, isn't it? Somehow, she's got you on her side. You're feeling sore because you think I'm taking advantage of her—*using* her!'

Morgan's eyes flicked up. 'And aren't you?'

'No!' Andrew pursed his lips. 'Oh, I'll admit, when she was younger, I didn't have much time for her, but when Cherry left me——'

'. . . you decided to realise your investment,' finished Morgan dispassionately, and the other man had the grace to look shamefaced.

'It wasn't like that,' he muttered, removing a pen from the onyx holder on his desk and twisting it round in his fingers. 'In any case, she can go back to the island if it means that much to her. I can't stop her. She's over eighteen.'

Morgan regarded him warily. 'And her allowance?'

'That will continue as before, of course. What do you take me for?'

Morgan frowned. 'Why?'

'Why what?'

'Why are you willing for her to go back to the island now, when you wouldn't even consider it before?'

Andrew pressed his hands down on the desk and got to his feet. 'I—didn't realise she—or you—felt so strongly about it.'

Morgan looked sceptical. 'Didn't you?'

'No. Dammit, Morgan, if that's what it takes for you to stay on at Forsyth's, I'll give her the house on the island, if you like.'

Morgan's pulse quickened. 'What did you say?'

'You heard me.'

'But I understood you needed her here.'

'I thought so, too.' Andrew spread his hands. 'I may have been a bit—premature.'

Morgan bent his head. 'You're thinking of getting married again, and Holly might be an encumbrance,' he said heavily. 'I am being obtuse. I should have realised at once.'

'That's not entirely true.' Andrew made a rueful

gesture. 'After three unsuccessful marriages, can you blame me?' He paused, and then continued, 'But, what would you say if I told you I was thinking of asking Alison to act as my hostess when necessary. I realised, while you were away, that having an older woman at my side is a definite advantage. I mean, when Cherry and I were together, she was always having to fend off passes from men I didn't want to offend.' He grimaced. 'Men like Lloyd Susman and Frank Disley for example. I had to grit my teeth when they were around, touching her with their greedy little hands! It made me sick!'

Morgan absorbed what the other man was saying with a feeling of distaste. 'You wouldn't have objected to subjecting Holly to the same treatment,' he pointed out grimly. 'So long as it suited you, of course.'

Andrew gasped. 'Hey, come on, Morgan,' he exclaimed, with an aggrieved air. 'I wouldn't have let a man like Susman anywhere near Holly. For heaven's sake, she may be twenty, but she's still only a kid! For all her youth, Cherry was a different kettle of fish. A different kettle of fish entirely.'

Morgan got to his feet now, and pushed his hands into his trouser pockets. Andrew's words had rekindled all his own anger and self-recrimination, and he could just imagine how Andrew would react if he told him the real reason he wanted to leave Forsyth's.

'Look,' he said shortly. 'I've got to go. So long as you're still employing me, there's work that has to be done.' He moved round his chair, and edged his way towards the door. 'We'll talk again later, hmm? When we have more time.'

Andrew put out a hand as if to stop him, and then allowed it to fall again. 'You won't—well, you won't do anything irrevocable without consulting me first, will you?' he pleaded. 'Surely you owe me that much. After all these years.'

'Okay.' Morgan reached for the handle of the door. 'I won't do anything before we've had another chance to talk.' He broke off, and then added cautiously, 'About Holly: are you going to tell her what's going on? I think she ought to know.'

'You tell her,' said Andrew swiftly. 'Give her a ring at home. Ask her to have dinner with you. I know she'd like that. Holly always did have a soft spot for you, Morgan. You know that.'

In fact, Morgan did try to ring Holly that afternoon, but without any success. Mrs Percy could only tell him that she was out—she didn't know where—and could she give her a message when she got back?

'No. Don't bother,' said Morgan, half afraid the girl might get the wrong idea. Had it not been for the fact that he knew Andrew was likely to put off telling Holly what was going on, he would never have agreed to act as mediator, and the last thing he wanted was to create the wrong impression.

For himself, Andrew's abrupt volte-face had caused him to have second thoughts. In spite of Andrew's arrogance and selfishness, they had worked together too long for Morgan to dismiss their relationship without cause. If Holly did decide to go back to the island, it would make a mockery of the gesture he was making, and wouldn't it be simpler to buy a house here in London and let Jeff and Jon choose where they wanted to live?

Andrew rang again, just before he left the office that evening. 'I don't want to rush you, but have you given my offer any serious consideration?' he probed anxiously, and Morgan sighed.

'Yes, I've given it consideration,' he said propping the receiver behind his ear, to enable him to go on packing his briefcase as they talked. 'Give me some time, Andrew. I'm not about to jump on the next flight to Boston. I'll let you know in a couple of days. After I've had a chance to talk to the boys.'

'Ah, yes. They're due back at the end of the week, aren't they?' Andrew acknowledged thoughtfully. 'Which reminds me, did you speak to Holly?'

'Not yet,' replied Morgan flatly. 'But I haven't forgotten.'

'Good. Good.' Andrew was evidently trying to think of something else to say, and Morgan clicked his briefcase closed, and removed the receiver from beneath his ear.

'Until tomorrow then,' he said pointedly, and Andrew gave a grunt of resignation.

'I meant what I said about that rise,' he added swiftly. 'I don't know why I didn't think of it before. Five per cent more than Shafer's are offering you.'

'All right, Andrew.' Morgan nodded. 'I appreciate it.' And without giving his employer time to make any further comment, he firmly replaced the receiver.

The worst of the rush hour was over when Morgan emerged on to Horseferry Road. It was an easy matter to hire a taxi, and he sank back against the worn leather upholstery with a feeling of total weariness. It was more than just being tired. He had been tired before without experiencing this awful sense of depression. It was the way he had felt the night before, after he had left Andrew's house in Hampstead, and he had the unpleasant conviction that he would go on feeling this way, until he got Holly out of his system—if he ever did!

During the day, he was able to cope with it. His work was demanding, and there were always other people to see, to talk to, to distract his mind from the ultimate abyss that thinking of Holly created. He knew she was not for him; he had accepted that any relationship between them was unthinkable; but, when he was alone, he could not prevent her image from tormenting him.

He wanted her. He could not deny that. He had only to think of her for the stirring heat to invade his loins. *God*, he thought angrily, he was like a sex-starved youth, lusting after his first date! It was ludicrous! It wasn't as if he had lived a celibate life. Since he and Alison split up, there had been several women only too willing to satisfy his normal instincts, but this was the first time he had ever felt like this. He could hardly remember how he had felt about Alison when they got married. There had been no grand passion, he knew that. They had gone out together for over a year before they got engaged, and then marriage had been the natural progression. People got married in those days. They didn't live together first, to see if it worked. He doubted the outcome would have been any different if they had. The cracks in their relationship had taken too long to split apart.

He blamed himself. He always had. Even though it was Alison herself who had caused him to take the irrevocable step of moving out of the house. He could still remember the disgust he had felt that day, when he had arrived back unexpectedly early from a trip abroad, and discovered Alison with another man. But that was all he had felt—disgust. Not pain; nor violence; nor jealousy; just disgust. And that was when he had realised that anything he had felt for her was long dead, strangled by the continuous pressure of her demands.

His feelings for Holly, therefore, had taken him completely by surprise. He had begun to believe he was in control of his destiny, that perhaps he deserved the claims that he was cold-blooded which Alison threw at him from time to time. He had not been worried. He had always liked women, and generally they liked him. He enjoyed sex, and he would never have believed there was anything more. But now he knew differently, and the unguarded claws of blind passion were tearing him to pieces.

By the time the taxi dropped him outside the block of flats in Queen's Terrace, Morgan's spirits had sunk to an all-time low. As the lift transported him to the eighth floor, he was mentally making an inventory of the contents of his drinks cupboard, and he decided, with a savage grimace, that unless he was prepared to walk to the nearest off-licence he would have to drink brandy instead of Scotch this evening.

To his relief, there was no one about in the corridor, and he reached his door without incident. But, as he inserted his key in the lock, he thought he could detect the sound of voices inside, and he guessed, with a feeling of resignation, that his neighbour had decided to come and check on the casserole. She invariably put the radio on when she was in the flat, though, and it was just possible that she had forgotten to turn it off that morning. Morgan prayed that that was what had happened. He didn't much feel like being civil to anyone in his present frame of mind.

The door opened into an oblong hallway, from which doors led into his bedroom and its adjoining bathroom. A third door opened into the living room, the kitchen being only an extension of the living area, and it was from the living room that the sounds were coming; not a radio at all, but voices: his sons' voices interspersed with a woman's tones.

The female voice was familiar, but Morgan was in no state to identify it before he thrust open his living-room door. In the back of his mind was the angry suspicion that it must be Alison, that somehow she had inveigled her way into his flat, and he was furious. But the reality that met his savage gaze was so much different, he could only stand there in the doorway, at the mercy of his raw emotions. It was not Alison who was seated on the sofa, sharing a pot of tea with Jon and Jeff, but Holly, and, if the laughter he had interrupted was anything to go by, they were managing perfectly well without him.

CHAPTER TEN

'Hɪ, Dad!'

'Hello, Dad!'

The two boys spoke in unison, and Holly was glad of their uncomplicated greeting to give her time to recover her composure. She had been existing on a high plane of tension ever since Morgan's next-door neighbour let them into the flat, and although she had been anticipating Morgan's arrival, nothing had prepared her for the sudden hollowing of her stomach when he opened the door and looked at her. She didn't know how he felt. Morgan was adept at concealing his real feelings, and it had taken more than a little nerve on her part to make this unwarranted intrusion. But she had to see him. She had to talk to him. And, as going to the office was out of the question, she had had no other alternative.

Morgan came into the room now, dropping his briefcase on to a chair by the door, and sliding his hands into the pockets of his trousers. Sometime, in the lift, perhaps, he had unfastened the top button of his shirt and pulled his tie a few inches away from his collar. The less-than-immaculate appearance made him more approachable somehow, but his expression was constrained, and she longed to go and massage the tension out of his shoulders.

'I thought you two weren't due back for another three days,' Morgan said now, dealing with his sons first, and, watching them together, Holly knew a different kind of emotion. Although the boys were twins, they were not identical. Jeff, she now knew, was the shorter of the two. He was stocky, too, and she guessed he resembled Alison's side of the family. Jon, however, was his father's son. Tall and thin, still with the adolescent angularity of youth, which made his wrists project too far from the sleeves of his sweater, and his trousers hang too loosely on his bony hips. But give him another three or four years, she reflected, and those limbs would acquire Morgan's supple muscularity. Already, she had learned, he possessed his father's humour and his self-assurance; all he needed was to gain his father's strength.

It was Jon who answered now, explaining that the course had had to be curtailed, due to the fact that so many of the young people had been ill. 'The seas were pretty rough,' he added, casting a sympathetic glance in his brother's direction. 'Jeff's been really sick. I don't think he ever wants to see a ship again.'

'I don't,' confirmed Jeff fervently, revealing his own sense of humour. 'God—I wanted to die sometimes, I felt so bloody.'

Morgan winced a little at his son's language, but he didn't embarrass him by commenting on it, and Holly was relieved. It wasn't important how they described their trip. The important thing was that they had come to tell their father all about it.

'So,' said Morgan now, 'have you been home? Does your mother know you're back?'

'No. Not yet.' Jon grimaced. 'We did go to Wimbledon, Dad, honestly, but Mum wasn't home, so we just dumped our stuff in the garage and came on here. That was how we met Holly.'

Holly wondered what Morgan was thinking right then. His expression was unreadable, and she wished she had a more credible answer for the question she was sure was to come.

But before Morgan could say anything, Jeff took up

the story. 'You don't mind us being here, do you, Dad?' he exclaimed. 'Your next-door neighbour—Mrs Latimer, isn't it?—she let us in.' He grimaced. 'It was quite amusing really. We were all hanging about outside the flat, when she came home after collecting her kids from school. She recognised us, of course, but she didn't know Holly. Anyway, when Holly found out who we were, she had to identify herself.' His eyes narrowed. 'Nice surprise, hmm?'

'Hmm.'

Morgan was non-committal, and Holly wondered what he really thought of her intervention. Of course, had she known the twins were likely to be here, she wouldn't have come, but, having rung Morgan's bell, she had been obliged to say who she was. Even then, she had not known the twins were just back from a sailing holiday. That had come out afterwards, after she had offered to make them a cup of tea.

Of the two, Jeff had been the most forthcoming, though she sensed a certain ingenuity in his manner. He was evidently curious about her relationship with his father, and although they had both made her laugh in recounting their adventures, with Jeff she suspected it was a means to an end.

'Holly's been telling us about your accident,' Jeff said now, and Holly cringed at the way he made it sound. In actual fact, she had said very little, except to excuse her presence there on the grounds of coming to enquire how their father was, but Morgan was not to know that.

'Really?' he said now, making his way across the room to a cabinet which proved to contain drinks. Intercepting Holly's distressed gaze, Jon intervened.

'She said you'd had a fall from a horse, while you were staying with her,' he put in evenly. 'How did it happen? I didn't even know you could ride.'

'Evidently I can't,' responded Morgan drily, pouring himself a measure of some amber-coloured liquid. Scotch or brandy: Holly couldn't be sure which. 'Unfortunately, it meant I had to spend rather longer on the island than I had intended.'

'Unfortunately!' echoed Jeff, with a sidelong glance at Holly. 'That's hardly the way I'd have described it.'

Morgan shrugged. 'No, well, I'm sure you would have enjoyed it,' he conceded. 'You could have water-skied to your heart's content, and I imagine the conditions for scuba-diving are excellent.'

'Didn't you do any scuba-diving, Dad?' asked Jon eagerly. 'You were quite good at it when we were in Mauritius a couple of years ago.'

'I'm afraid I'm getting a bit old for that sort of thing,' retorted Morgan crisply, and Holly guessed his statement was directed at her. 'I did manage to get in a day's sailing while I was there. That's more my scene than all these physical pursuits.'

'Even so . . .' Jeff seemed determined to provoke his father's anger. 'I bet Holly could have shown you all the best places to dive. Hasn't she been living out there for two years? Hell, I bet she's a whizz at any kind of watersport.'

'Yes.' Morgan inclined his head. 'Well, she is more your age than mine, Jeff,' he essayed bleakly. 'Now—I suggest we consider dinner, don't you?'

While Holly absorbed the impact of Morgan's implied rebuff, Jon got to his feet. 'I don't think we ought to stay for dinner, Dad,' he declared firmly, ignoring his twin's gasp of protest. 'Really, we haven't seen Mum yet, and I think we ought to let her know we're back. We can come round tomorrow and tell you all about the trip. If you're going to be here, of course.'

'I'll be here, Jon,' answered Morgan swiftly, but Jeff was definitely put out.

'There *are* phones,' he told his brother aggressively. 'Why don't we stay and have dinner with Dad? Mum will most likely be out anyway.'

Jon gave him a speaking look, and Jeff hunched his shoulders resentfully. 'Okay, okay,' he muttered. 'I know when I'm not wanted. I just thought Dad might have wanted to spend a little time with us, as we've been away for over two weeks.'

'Look, I'd better be going, too,' murmured Holly unhappily, standing up herself. 'I—I only came to see—to see how you were, Mr—er—Morgan——'

'Don't leave on our account,' Jon interrupted her quietly. 'We really do have to go. Whatever this tactless oaf says!'

He hauled his twin to his feet and, in the fuss of their departure, Holly had no further chance to make her own farewells. 'I hope we see you again,' said Jon, as he reached the door, and Jeff pulled a mocking face. 'Soon,' he added as Jon propelled him outside, and Morgan followed them into the hall leaving Holly on her own.

Left to herself, Holly started to sit down again, and then changed her mind and remained standing. She had been nervous when she arrived here, but not half so nervous as she was now, and she pushed her hands into the pockets of her leather jacket to hide her unsteadiness.

The skirt of her suit seemed absurdly short suddenly, ending just above her knee and exposing the slender length of her leg. But it was the warmest suit she possessed, having been bought on one of her infrequent trips to St Thomas; and, having been made in New York, its style was unmistakable. She had wanted to look good—to look mature; but Morgan had succeeded, with Jeff's help, in accentuating the gulf between them once again.

To fill in the time, she tried to take an interest in her surroundings, but she had already had plenty of opportunity to study Morgan's living room. It was quite attractive, with its plain cream walls, hung with framed art nouveau posters, and the squashy suede sofas that faced one another across the wide expanse of off-white carpet. The living area was separated from the small service kitchen by a screen of dark wood, upon whose shelves paperbacks and magazines jostled side by side with a couple of heavy bronze figurines and a Swiss cheese plant. The casserole, which had been on the point of burning when Holly arrived at the flat, was sitting on top of the oven, giving off a faint, but delicious, odour of cooked meat. She had guessed Mrs Latimer used the key in her possession for other purposes than to let in unexpected visitors, and she wondered with a pang whether there was a *Mr* Latimer.

The outer door slammed at that moment, and Holly tensed. She decided, belatedly, that she ought to have been sitting down, but it was too late to do anything about it now. A more sophisticated woman—a woman like Alison, for example—would have removed her jacket and made herself at home, but Holly had not prepared her approach. She was here; and she was nervous; that was as far as she could go. How she should face Morgan was not something she could anticipate.

Morgan came into the room at that moment, his dark face revealing no element of welcome. Instead, he went across to where he had left the bottle of what she now saw to be brandy, and poured himself a generous measure before facing her again.

'I assume Mrs Percy gave you my message after all,' he remarked bleakly, and Holly blinked.

'Your message?'

'I phoned,' said Morgan, taking a swallow of the liquid in his glass. 'I should have had more sense!'

Holly moistened her dry lips. 'I—I got no message,' she stammered uncertainly, and Morgan's expression darkened.

'Then what the hell are you doing here?' he snapped, his grey eyes spearing her like chips of ice. 'For Christ's sake, I thought I was to blame for this crazy invasion! Do you mean to say you came here without a reason?'

'No.' Holly winced. 'I mean—I did—I *do*—have a reason.' She took her hands out of her pockets and they flexed and balled against her thighs.

'Not that shit about wanting to find out about my health!' swore Morgan furiously. 'I don't believe that!'

'Not—not that,' exclaimed Holly quickly. 'But I had to say something in front of your sons, and——'

'Oh, God! The twins!' muttered Morgan, overriding her explanations. 'You do realise they'll tell Alison about this, don't you? And she, of course, will find some way to drop it into conversation with your father, and then there really will be hell to pay!'

'Why?'

'Why?' Morgan took another mouthful of his brandy. 'You are joking, of course! Can you imagine how your father will react when he discovers you've been here? I just might have swung it, if Mrs Percy had told you I called. But if she didn't . . .'

'I haven't been home,' said Holly simply. 'I—I left the house this morning, intending to call you at the office. But then I changed my mind. I spent most of the day in the British Museum. I came here when I thought you'd be home.'

Morgan shook his head. 'Well, I think you'd better leave right now. How did you get here? By taxi? If I call a mini-cab right away, you might just make it back before Alison has a chance to make something of it.'

'No,' Holly stood her ground. 'And don't call a taxi because I didn't come that way. My old Mini was still in the garage. Tom keeps it in good working order, so I used that. It's parked in Queen's Gardens.'

Morgan finished his drink and put the glass aside. 'Then I suggest you go and collect it,' he advised her harshly. 'You can always make some excuse about getting stuck in a traffic jam. Your father may not even be home yet. He was still in the office when I left.'

'No.'

Morgan expelled his breath heavily. 'Yes.'

Holly was intimidated, but she resisted the urge to obey him. 'Don't you want to know why I came?' she protested desperately. 'Morgan, please! At least, tell me why you rang me. You must have had a reason.'

'That can wait,' said Morgan shortly, gesturing towards the door. 'Come on, Holly, I've had a hard day. I'll be in touch later in the week. I promise.'

Holly shook her head. 'You really dislike me, don't you?' she exclaimed, realising she had probably jeopardised any chance of an understanding between them by coming here, and Morgan allowed his breath to escape him on a weary sigh.

'No,' he said succinctly. 'No, I don't dislike you, Holly. I just think your coming here was ill-advised. Whatever you want to say to me could have just as easily been said at the office. Or whenever I called you, as I've just told you I did.'

'But I didn't know you were likely to call me, did I?' she protested, taking a few involuntary steps towards him, as if to emphasise her point. 'After—after what you said last night, I didn't think there was any likelihood of you seeking me out.'

Morgan's mouth tightened. 'After what was said last night, you should have had more sense than to come here,' he retorted, grimly.

Holly pursed her lips. 'Why? I mean, aside from the fact that bumping into Jon and Jeff wasn't exactly what

I had in mind, what harm have I done?'

'Holly, a girl of your age doesn't usually visit a man of my age in his flat——'

'Oh, *age*! That's all you think about!' she declared impatiently. 'Why do you always bring up my age? I'm not a child! I'm an adult! We're *two* adults—and I see no reason why we can't have a civil conversation——'

'Don't you?' Morgan's mouth twisted, and her heart flipped a beat at the sudden aggression in his eyes.

'No,' she said, after a moment, still hoping to reason with him. 'Morgan——' She took the steps that brought her within arm's length of his unyielding figure. 'Morgan, won't you at least tell me if what your—your—*Alison* said was true? You can't be thinking of leaving Forsyth's. I—well—my father wouldn't let you.'

'Your father couldn't stop me,' responded Morgan flatly.

'But why? Why?'

'Don't you know?' he demanded with some heat, but when she shook her head, all the anger seemed to drain out of him. 'Then you should,' he answered heavily, stretching out his hand and trailing his knuckles down the tender skin of her cheek. The bruise was finally fading and, as the swelling had gone down, make-up had almost disguised the injury. But it was incredibly sensitive, the more so because it was Morgan's hand that was stroking her flesh. 'Because of you,' he added at last, allowing his hand to fall to his side. 'Now will you get out of here?'

Holly's breathing had been suspended, but now she took several unsteady gulps of air. 'You mean—you mean——'

'I mean that this relationship isn't healthy; for either of us,' he muttered harshly. 'It wasn't healthy on the island, and it sure as hell isn't healthy here! Just go home, will you? Your father will be wondering where you are.'

Holly ignored his words, gazing at him as if she had never seen him before, and Morgan grew impatient. With a gesture of frustration, he abandoned any attempt to reason with her and, as if desperate for the relief alcohol could bring, he started towards the brandy.

His action brought Holly to her senses and, without stopping to consider the wisdom of what she was about to do, she went after him, sliding her arms round him from behind, and pressing her face against his back.

'Holly, for Christ's sake!'

The anger, which had been lying dormant since Morgan had succeeded in controlling his temper, erupted into violence. His hands clamped down on her wrists, tearing them away from his body, as he swung round to face her. His eyes were glittering dangerously, and his lean face was taut with emotion. But it was not the tender ardour she had anticipated. It was raw, naked passion, and her heart pounded wildly at the realisation that she had pushed him too far.

Something of her feelings must have shown in her face for, as if unable to sustain his anger against her, Morgan's hands gentled on her slender bones. Then, again with a gesture almost of defeat, he brought her wrists to his lips, and fired her with the probing caress of his tongue.

'Morgan . . . she breathed, hardly daring to say even his name, and he lifted his head and looked at her.

It was a devastating appraisal, an abrasive assault on her senses, and her whole body seemed suffused in heat as he drew her almost resistingly towards him. Then, as his hands slipped over her shoulders, sliding the leather jacket down her arms and from there to the floor, he lowered his mouth to the pulse palpitating at her nape.

She trembled, and Morgan's arms closed around her.

With infinite skill, he moulded her quivering body to the supple strength of his own, and then, allowing his lips to trail up her neck, he found the yielding sweetness of her mouth.

Holly's lips parted instinctively beneath that searching pressure. She had desperately wanted him to kiss her, and the eager warmth of his tongue was a welcome invader. Her hands, which had lingered uncertainly at his waist when he released them, now slid up inside his jacket to his neck, and her fingers probed inside the collar of his shirt.

The kiss deepened, and any hope Morgan might have had that by kissing her he might expunge the needs inside him was quickly dispelled. On the contrary, when he felt her fingers persuasively easing his jacket from his shoulders, he willingly facilitated her efforts, and the gentleness of his touch gave way to an urgent possession.

Holly's head was spinning, but when he tore his mouth away to seek the peachy softness of her cheeks and the delicate curve of her jawline, she soon became impatient. Twining her fingers in the hair at his nape, she brought his mouth back to hers, using her tongue to tease him now, so that presently he groaned in hungry protest.

As if his strength was weakening, he sought the creamy suede sofa behind him and, lowering his weight on to its yielding softness, he pulled her down on top of him. The force of her willingness to comply drove him on to his back and, as her limbs tangled with his, she felt the swelling muscle between his legs.

'Ah, Holly,' he muttered, his hands on her buttocks, pressing her down on to his undoubted maleness. And then, with her skirt riding up to her hips, he turned her on to her back, covering her slender length with his lean body.

Just for a moment, as he looked down into her flushed face, Holly sensed he knew a brief compunction. His hands stilled and she felt the tension stiffening his body. But her frantic fingers at his throat, tugging his tie aside and parting the remaining buttons of his shirt, drew an almost involuntary response, and when she reached up and put her lips to his, he hadn't the will to break even that tenuous union.

With a groan of defeat, he let her pull him down to her again, and now his lips crushed hers with their vehemence, and his tongue in her mouth drove her far beyond the point of knowing what was right and what was wrong. Her legs, weak and tremulous from the force of the emotions he was evoking inside her, fell apart almost without her being aware of it, and she fretted at the barriers that still kept them apart. She wanted to be able to touch the rest of him, as she was able to touch the muscled strength of his chest, bared beneath her hands. She wanted them to be closer, much closer, and she twisted a little restlessly when his laboured breathing revealed he was still struggling to regain control.

'I want you,' she breathed unsteadily, though in all honesty she had no clear idea of what she was inviting. Nevertheless, she knew she had never felt this way before, and her instincts told her that this was right. It didn't matter if he hurt her; she had suspected for years that she was not the type of girl who could find real pleasure in sex, believing, quite philosophically, that that was why she had remained a virgin when all her friends had not. But for the first time in her life that distinction was no longer desirable to her, and she desperately wanted to prove to Morgan she was not the child he thought her.

'You don't know what you want,' Morgan groaned harshly and, as if her words had restored a measure of his sanity, he pushed himself up on his hands, so that only the unmistakable thrust of his arousal still pulsed against her thigh.

'I do, I do,' she protested fiercely and, with a sensuality she had not known she possessed, her hands went automatically to the studded fastenings of her shirt, tearing them apart and exposing the creamy fullness of her breasts to his tormented eyes. Swollen and pointed, they were scarcely contained by the lacy bra that held them, and with trembling fingers she unhooked the front fastening, so that the rosy pink nipples nudged his midriff.

'Dear God, *Holly*!' he muttered, unable to drag his eyes away, and with increasing confidence, her hands went to the belt of his trousers, loosening the buckle and reaching for the zip. But when she would have propelled it downwards, his fingers came to cover hers, and he sat back on his heels, pressing her hands against him.

'Don't you want me?' she whispered, anxiously now, and Morgan tipped back his head in agony.

'Yes, I want you,' he grated roughly, his eyes drawn back to her uncertain face. 'So long as you know what you're doing.'

Holly moistened her lips. 'Why shouldn't I?' she countered. 'I—you're not the first man I've made love with.'

A spasm of emotion crossed his face: relief; anger; distaste; she couldn't be sure which. But beneath her hands, the throbbing hunger of his body demanded release and, with insistent fingers, she captured the metal tag of the zip.

He groaned as his maleness spilled into her hands, but there was no further talk of the moral rights and wrongs of their need for one another. With lithe dexterity, Morgan divested himself of his shirt and trousers, and then, while her hands ran possessively over his lean muscular shoulders, he drew her skirt down over her hips. The sensuous brush of his lips against her navel as he slid off her tights was disturbing, but she managed not to show too much alarm when he followed the removal of her tights with his tongue. Even so, to feel those featherlight kisses skimming the inner curve of her thigh brought a wave of heat to moisten her skin, and she quivered a little anxiously when his fingers probed her sweetness.

However, the sensations he evoked soon dispelled all but an urgent need to feel him in her. His size was daunting, but with his mouth devouring hers once again, and the delicious abrasion of the hair on his body sensitising her skin, she was in no state to probe her fears too deeply. Evidently the moistness of her skin was quite normal, she decided, as with increasing urgency Morgan covered her face and neck with kisses, and when his teeth took possession of one swollen nipple after the other, her hips rose towards him in unknowing invitation.

The heat of his flesh as it sought her inner warmth was like a flame seeking to ignite her. But it was hard, too, and insistent, and she felt her muscles tensing, just when she wanted to relax. Morgan tensed, too, and her hands on his hips felt the sudden bunching of his muscles. But he did not withdraw. Although she knew a momentary sense of panic that he might have guessed her secret, his next action proved her wrong. With a sigh of satisfaction, he thrust himself into her, and her breath escaped on a squeaky cry.

If she had allowed his mouth to go on possessing hers with its hungry intimacy, Morgan might never have suspected what had happened—or so she thought. But at the moment his flesh tore her tender membrane aside, she had jerked back from him, the sob rising in her throat. And in the aftermath of his invasion, she had been unable to prevent the involuntary betrayal.

'I should choke you, do you know that?' he muttered, burying his face in the hollow of her neck and breathing rather raggedly. 'You lied to me. Didn't you realise I would hurt you?'

Now that the worst was over, Holly didn't want him to talk. 'You didn't hurt me,' she protested, winding her arms around his neck. 'And it feels good, doesn't it? You're not sorry we're together?'

'Sorry?' groaned Morgan roughly, lifting his head so that she could see his face. 'I just think you're crazy, that's all!'

'I love you,' she breathed, pressing tentative little kisses all along his jawline and up to the curve of his harsh mouth. 'I wanted to please you. And I have— haven't I?'

'To please me?' he echoed, his breath catching in his throat. 'Oh, God, Holly, you please me!' he conceded, almost savagely, and then, as if unable to prevent himself, he began to move.

Holly panicked, sure he was about to leave her after all, and her legs, coiling innocently around his back, caused him to plunge even more deeply into her silken web. 'Holly, don't make me do this,' he muttered, his tongue darting ever more deeply into her mouth, but he was powerless to resist. Just as Holly was beginning to enjoy the sensuous thrust of his body, just as a strange, kindling fire dispelled the pain and began to build inside her, just as she began to believe that perhaps she had been wrong about herself all along, Morgan uttered a cry of anguish, and slumped on top of her. Disappointed and confused, Holly felt a flooding warmth between her legs, and then a depressing anti-climax as Morgan rolled over on to his back.

So, she thought bleakly, she had been right. She was

sexless, sterile, frigid—all the epithets young men had flung at her since she first started dating. That was why she had never been tempted to allow any man to make love to her. Why she had found it so easy to repel their fervent advances.

And yet, it hadn't been like that with Morgan. From the beginning, she had wanted him to kiss her, to touch her, to make love to her. She had welcomed his nearness, had revelled in the strength of his lean body and courted the sensuous possession of his mouth. She had actually seduced him into believing she was a woman, just to feel his flesh against hers. And now, she had proved that even with the man she loved she could not respond. She was an empty shell, a husk; a useless vacuum, incapable of giving anything but facile promises.

With a suppressed sob, she turned her head and looked at him. This should have been the happiest moment of her life, she thought, and instead it was the most miserable. She loved him—dear *God*! there was no doubt about that. Even just looking at him lying there, his firm, muscled body exposed in unashamed beauty, she badly wanted to touch him, which seemed totally at variance with her inability to respond. The knowledge that they had been as close—physically, if not spiritually—as any man and woman could be was a tantalising perception, and she wondered, with an urgency born of desperation, whether she might not have expected too much.

Morgan moved at that moment and turned his head, his eyes meeting Holly's startled gaze before she could avoid it. She didn't want him to look at her. She didn't want him to remember how unresponsive she had been. But his grey eyes imprisoned hers with gripping penetration and, although she brought her hands up to cover her body, she could not look away.

Morgan groaned then and, preventing the involuntary urge she had to scramble off the couch and away from him, he turned on to his side and put his mouth against her shoulder.

'I'm sorry,' he breathed huskily, his words bringing a frown of worry to her troubled brow, and she blinked.

'You're—you're sorry?'

She didn't understand, and with infinite gentleness Morgan removed her hands from her breasts and allowed his tongue to stroke the still taut nipples. 'Yes, sorry,' he said, tugging at the swollen peaks with warm insistence. 'I know I should have been more gentle, but I wanted you too much. And you didn't exactly help the situation by responding as you did.'

Holly trembled. 'I don't understand——'

'I know.' Morgan's mouth twisted slightly. 'And I'm not explaining things very well. Let's just say, you made me lose my head. I can't remember that happening before. Which proves what you do to me.'

Holly moved her head from side to side. 'It was my fault.'

'What was your fault?' Morgan lifted his head.

'Your—I mean—my lack of response.' Holly flushed scarlet. 'It's me. I—I'm not the kind of girl who—well, who can enjoy—enjoy——'

'What are you talking about?'

'Making love,' she appended firmly. 'I'm—I'm cold; frigid——'

'Like hell,' muttered Morgan harshly, stopping her words with angry impatience. 'What in God's name are you telling me? I just blew the most perfect relationship I've ever had with any woman, and you make it some inane interpretation of your own deficiencies!'

'It's true.'

'It's not true,' he retorted savagely, moving closer, so that Holly was able to feel him against her hip.

Capturing her hand, he pulled it down between them, letting her experience the stirring length of him against her palm. 'That,' he said, somewhat thickly, 'that is what you do to me. I never intended to compound my sins, but this is something I've got to do. You're not frigid, my love, you're quite the opposite. And now, just to set the record straight, I'm going to prove it.'

'But, didn't you——?'

'A few minutes ago? Yes, I did,' said Morgan, his voice a mixture of humour, compassion, and self-derision. 'But I want you again. That's how *un*responsive you are! Only this time, it will be different. I promise you that.'

CHAPTER ELEVEN

AND it was different. With infinite tenderness and innate skill, Morgan used his mouth and tongue to bring her confused senses back to vibrant life, and this time, when he penetrated the tightly knit muscles that opened for him, there was no pain, only intense satisfaction.

But even that was nothing compared to what came after. With her head flung back and her legs curled tightly about him, she felt her breathing quicken as Morgan thrust urgently against her. He plunged his body into hers in an ever-increasing rhythm, and she found herself meeting his demands with an urgency of her own.

It couldn't go on, she thought incoherently, as he drove her towards an unimagined culmination, but the incredible happened, and it did. And then, just when she felt as if her body could not absorb any more pleasure, she was swung out into space, detached, suspended, caught in a hectic swirl of ecstasy that seemed the nearest thing to spiritual—and physical—gratification she could imagine. Her breath escaped in little gasps, as she gulped frantically for air, and only as she floated back to earth did she realise her nails were digging into Morgan's shoulders. Morgan himself had reached a similar peak only seconds behind her. She had felt his shuddering climax as he spilled himself inside her, and she had known an overwhelming sense of tenderness for the beauty he had shown her.

Holly moved now, but it was only to nestle closer to him, and her whispered, 'I never knew,' was breathed against his damp skin.

It was when her fingers slid possessively over his shoulders that they came away smeared with blood, and she caught her breath. 'I've hurt you,' she exclaimed, half afraid of what she had done, and Morgan's eyes flickered as he gave her a half ironic smile.

'I'll survive,' he told her flatly, but then, as if realising how closely she was still coiled against his body, he shifted abruptly and pushed himself up, threading long fingers through the tumbled darkness of his hair.

Her involuntary protest fell on deaf ears as he got off the couch, and his words when he spoke were cold and dispassionate. 'I believe we've exploded the myth of your frigidity anyway,' he remarked, pulling on the trousers he had discarded earlier. 'Only I need a drink. It's not every day I can be accused of seducing a virgin!'

Holly made a sound of denial and scrambled up, too. 'You didn't seduce me,' she protested, drawing up her knees and encircling them with her arms. 'I—I seduced you. Or at least—I tried to.'

Morgan grimaced. 'Who would believe that?' he demanded, zipping up his trousers. 'Not your father, that's for sure.' His face darkened ominously. 'Okay, Holly, you've got me over a barrel. What is it you want from me? Revenge—or an affair?'

Holly quivered. 'Don't talk like that!'

'Why not?' Morgan was bitter. 'There's not much I can do to stop you, is there?'

Holly gasped. 'You could say you loved me,' she declared tremulously. 'I love you. I think I always have.'

Morgan uttered an oath. 'You don't know what you're talking about!'

'I do!' Realising the limitations of her present situation, Holly hurried awkwardly into her shirt and the tight leather skirt that matched her jacket. She didn't bother with the bra. Her idea was to simply cover herself in the shortest time possible. Then she, too, got to her feet and faced him bravely. 'I love you, Morgan,' she repeated huskily. 'And—and if you meant what you said about—about leaving Forsyth's because of me, you don't have to. Oh—I know with my father being interested in Alison——'

'You know about that?'

'. . . it's difficult for you,' she continued, ignoring his interruption. 'But does it have to be a problem?'

'Holly——'

'No, listen to me! I—I don't expect anything of you. I realise, after one unsuccessful marriage, you might not want to commit yourself again——'

'Holly, stop this!' Morgan's face was contorted, and he thrust one hand through his hair before it came to rest at the nape of his neck. 'My relationship with Alison has nothing to do with how I feel about—about us!'

'No?'

'No!'

Holly moistened her lips. 'You're really not leaving Forsyth's because of her?'

Morgan's eyes narrowed. 'Who gave you that idea? Your father?'

'No.'

'Who then?'

'Maybe I thought of it for myself.'

'Did you?'

Holly bent her head. 'Alison said so,' she muttered unwillingly, and then winced when Morgan's fingers fastened round her arm.

'When?'

'Last night.'

'*When*—last night?'

'In the library. After dinner.' His grip was bruising, but Holly made no protest. 'While—while you and my father were still at the table.'

'My God!' Morgan's mouth compressed. 'So that's why you disappeared immediately after.' He gave an impatient grunt. 'You surely didn't believe her?'

'I thought I didn't.' Holly moistened her dry lips. 'Now I'm not so sure.'

Morgan groaned. 'Holly, you know as well as I do that if I stay in England—*this*—will go on.'

Holly trembled. 'Will it?'

The look of wide-eyed anticipation in her eyes was unmistakable and, with an oath, Morgan released her. 'Holly, you're twenty years of age——'

'Almost twenty-one!'

'. . . and you should be looking around for someone of your own——'

'If you say *age* again, I'll scream!' she interposed fiercely, and he shook his head.

'It's true, Holly.'

'I'm not interested in anyone of my own age,' she retorted huskily. And then, with great daring, she added, 'Are you?'

'What I want doesn't come into it.'

'Why not?' Gaining in confidence, she covered the space between them, only stopping when his hands fastened on her shoulders, keeping her at arm's length. 'You can't make my father an excuse any longer.'

'No?'

'No.' Holly hesitated. 'I mean—if you were prepared to take another job to get away from me, why not take another job to get away from him?'

Morgan grimaced. 'You make it sound so easy, don't you?'

'It is easy.'

'And what if your father had you made a ward of court, or something like that?'

'He couldn't do that. Could he?' Holly was confused, but then, glimpsing his wry expression, she exclaimed,

'Don't tease me! Morgan, please! You do care about me a little, don't you?'

'A little,' he conceded roughly. 'But there's something else.'

'What else?'

Morgan paused. 'Your father. We had a talk this morning. About you, among other things.'

'And?' She was anxious.

'And—he's offered to allow you to go back to the island, if you want to. No strings attached.'

Holly absorbed this in silence, and then she said quietly, 'Because of Alison, I suppose. Is he going to marry her?'

'Marry, no.' Morgan released her and she swayed a little unsteadily. 'Associate with, yes.'

'You mean—you mean——'

'I doubt if your father knows exactly what he means right now,' said Morgan drily. 'And knowing Alison, I daresay she'll have some say in the matter.' He took a breath. 'Do you mind?'

Holly hunched her shoulders. 'Did he tell you to tell me this?'

Her perception was acute and Morgan sighed. 'He thought it might come better from me. As I brought you to England.'

'You know that's not true.' Holly shook her head. 'He just hadn't the guts to tell me himself.' She looked up at him warily. 'I suppose it would solve both your problems, wouldn't it? My father's with Alison, and yours with me!'

Morgan was silent for so long, she thought he didn't intend to answer her at all, and her spirits plummeted. Of course, she thought bitterly, that would suit his purposes very well. Not only would she not be around to prove a distraction, but there would be no reason for him to leave Forsyth's.

Her breath catching in her throat, she turned away, looking about her blindly, searching for her shoes and jacket so that she could leave. Her tights she stuffed into the pocket of her jacket, but as she was rummaging about beside the sofa for her right shoe, Morgan came behind her, and jerked her up into his arms.

'All right,' he groaned harshly, pressing her back against him, burying his face in the scented hollow between her neck and her shoulder. 'Whatever I decide to do, we'll do together. I can't let you go. It may be madness, but I love you!'

Holly gasped. 'Do you mean it?' she breathed, covering the hands that spanned her stomach with her own, and allowing his fingers to take possession of hers.

'I mean it,' he averred, his tongue making sensuous little circles against her quivering flesh, and, turning her in his arms, he brought her mouth to his.

The sound of the doorbell was an infuriating distraction, and for a few moments Morgan ignored it. But then, putting Holly reluctantly away from him, he made an effort to stuff his shirt into his trousers. 'Mrs Latimer,' he told her softly. 'She's probably come for the casserole dish. I'll tell her I haven't had time to eat it yet.' He deposited a lingering kiss on her mouth, and then touched her cheek with a caressing finger. 'Don't go away.'

'I won't.'

Holly returned his kiss eagerly, and then, wrapping her arms about herself, she waited impatiently while he went to the door.

It wasn't Mrs Latimer. The familiar tones of her father came unmistakably to her ears and, with a feeling of apprehension and determination, she left the comparative safety of the living room and walked bravely into the hall beyond.

'. . . and, well, I was in the neighbourhood, and I

thought, what better chance for us to have a few private words——' Andrew was saying cajolingly, when he saw his daughter. Belatedly, Holly realised that her bare feet were a blatant indication of what had been going on, but she didn't care. As she had no intention of hiding anything from her father, there was no point in pretending.

Morgan, hearing his employer's sudden intake of breath, and sensing something was amiss, turned too, and Holly met his guarded gaze with tentative eyes. 'I heard voices,' she explained, going to him and looking up into his dark face. 'Shall I go?'

It was the moment of truth, and Morgan's mouth twisted into a smile that was for her alone. 'No,' he said softly, and anyone watching them could not be unaware of their complete rapport. 'I was just about to ask your father in for a drink. You don't have any objections, do you?'

Before she could answer, Andrew himself stepped into the flat, closing the door behind him with a heavy thud. 'We don't want to attract undue attention, do we?' he demanded, his voice harsh with shock and anger. 'My God! And I thought you were worried about Alison! How long has this little arrangement been going on?'

'Because you're Holly's father, I'll overlook that remark,' said Morgan flatly, his eyes cold with fury as he faced the older man. 'And this isn't an—arrangement, as you put it.' He slipped his arm around Holly's waist and pulled her against his hip. 'Your daughter and I are going to be married. With or without your permission. It's all the same to me.'

Some minutes later, Andrew was seated on the sofa in Morgan's flat swallowing his second brandy. It was one of the few occasions in his life when he was not in control of the situation, and it was evidently not a circumstance he relished.

However, time, and the brandy—and the knowledge that here was an opportunity to get his own way regarding Morgan's future—had served to make the news more palatable, and he was actually beginning to consider ways where it could be put to his advantage.

'You have to understand,' he was saying persuasively to the two people seated on the sofa opposite, 'the idea of you and Holly actually getting together hadn't even occurred to me, particularly as you were planning on leaving, Morgan.'

'Were?' The ice had gone out of Morgan's tone, but he was still wary. 'Don't you mean—*are*?'

'Are?' Andrew swallowed the remainder of his drink and put the glass aside. 'You can't still be thinking of leaving the company, Morgan! Not now you're going to be my son-in-law! Good heavens, the idea's quite absurd! This changes our relationship entirely.'

'That's what I'm afraid of,' said Morgan bleakly. 'Look, Andrew, you probably mean well, but Holly and I are not going to live in your pocket. Nor, might I add, is anyone going to accuse me of marrying her for your money!'

'As if anyone would!'

'Oh, they would,' said Morgan grimly, and as he looked again at Holly she thought how amazing it was that his expression could change so utterly in that split second. The coldness and the aggression he was showing towards her father was not there when he met her anxious gaze. Instead, his eyes softened and gentled, resting with sensual insistence on her nervously parted mouth, making her intolerably aware that already he was eager to make love to her again. For her part she had still not got over the delight of hearing Morgan say they were to be married. It was all like a dream, and one she had no wish to wake from.

'It doesn't matter what people say,' retorted Andrew now, impatient that anyone could distract Morgan's attention from himself. 'Look, boy, it would be madness to walk out, just when I'm on the point of retiring.'

Morgan gave a disbelieving laugh. 'You? Retiring? Come off it.'

'I mean it.' Andrew shifted a little restlessly in his seat. 'I'm sixty, Morgan. Old enough to know I haven't that many years of active life ahead of me. I want to enjoy those years, not spend them locked up in some stuffy boardroom.' He spread his hands. 'Do you realise what I'm offering you? The most marvellous opportunity of your career. You'd be a fool to turn it down.'

Morgan sighed. 'I need time to think about it.' He glanced once more at Holly. 'And to—talk it over with my fiancée. I'll let you know my decision later.'

Andrew clicked his tongue. 'How much later?'

'When we get back from our honeymoon,' declared Morgan steadily. 'You wouldn't deny me a honeymoon, would you, Andrew? Not after you've had so many . . .'

Exactly eight weeks later, Holly awoke to find her husband putting on his clothes. Shifting on to her back, her movements attracted his attention and, abandoning his attempt to knot his tie, he came swiftly over to the bed.

'Did I disturb you?' he murmured, looking down at her with lazily possessive eyes, and Holly moved invitingly across the bed, making room for him to sit next to her.

'What time is it?' she protested, capturing his wrist and holding his watch close to her eyes. It was light beyond the windows, but the illumination in the bedroom was muted by heavy damask curtains, and it was difficult to see the watch face.

'It's only eight o'clock,' Morgan told her gently, his eyes darkening as they rested in the creamy curve of her bare shoulder. 'Go back to sleep. There's no need for you to get up.'

Holly grimaced. 'Do you have to go back to work this morning? We've only been home a couple of days!'

'We've been home over a week,' Morgan corrected her ruefully. 'And while I have no intention of spending all my time in the office, I've got to make sure Parsons knows what he's doing.'

Holly dimpled. 'Your assistant?' she prompted teasingly, and he grimaced.

'My assistant,' he agreed, and then shook his head. 'Your father was certainly determined to get his own way, wasn't he?'

Holly's laughter was attractive. 'Well, at least it shows he has confidence in you,' she conceded, stroking featherlight fingers along his sleeve. 'And we did have a marvellous honeymoon, didn't we? In our own house?'

Morgan looked at her for a long disturbing minute, and then he nodded. 'At least it means the Fletchers don't have to worry any more,' he murmured. 'And whenever we feel the need to get away . . .'

'We can go to the island,' said Holly dreamily. 'It was a novel wedding present, wasn't it?'

Morgan pulled a wry face. 'I suppose so.'

'Well, at least the boys can use it whenever they want to,' said Holly practically. 'And this house, too, is better for them than the flat, isn't it?'

'Temporarily,' agreed Morgan, glancing round the green and gold luxury of their suite. 'But by the time your father and Alison get back, I want us to have a home of our own.'

'That won't be for months yet,' exclaimed Holly contentedly, her eyes dancing. 'Money does have its uses, don't you think?'

Morgan's mouth tilted. 'Can you honestly see your father spending six months on a world cruise?' he demanded sceptically. 'If I know Andrew, he'll be back within the next six weeks. Oh, I admit, it was good of him to take Alison with him, so that we could spend some time with the twins, alone, but he won't be able to stay away from Forsyth's for that length of time. Even if he has nominally handed over the reins to me, he'll want to be sure I don't make any mistakes.'

'Still, it is nice to be in charge, isn't it?' murmured Holly, finger-walking up his chest to curl her hands around his nape. 'You are happy, aren't you?'

'Happy?' Morgan uttered a smothered groan, and slid his arms around her. She was naked beneath the silk sheet, and his hands spread possessively over the downy curve of her hips. 'Happy is such an inadequate word to describe how I feel,' he told her huskily, against the silken flesh of her shoulder. 'Sometimes I wonder what I've done to deserve such happiness.'

'That's good.' Holly lifted her shoulder to facilitate his touch and shivered, but it was not with cold. 'Well—if you really must go . . .'

'You are a temptress, do you know that?' said Morgan roughly, lifting his head to look at her. 'You do realise Jon and Jeff are waiting for me, don't you?'

'They'll understand,' said Holly confidently, caressing his nape. 'Or at least, Jon will. He and I are good friends.'

'They both think you're something special, and you know it,' retorted Morgan unevenly. 'I know it's thanks to you they're even considering taking their exams. They'd practically given up the idea of school, before you came on the scene.'

'Well, I just pointed out that if they left home and got jobs, they'd have little time for learning to drive, or holidays; that sort of thing,' said Holly innocently, and Morgan shook his head.

'Bribery and corruption,' he told her. 'It never worked before.'

'Perhaps you just went about it the wrong way,' declared Holly mischievously. Then, after a moment's hesitation, she added, 'And, well—I don't think living with their mother was much fun.'

'Which is something else I have to thank you for,' put in Morgan softly. 'You handled Alison beautifully.'

'With my father's help,' said Holly modestly. She laughed. 'How did you manage without me?'

'I don't want to think about it,' exclaimed Morgan, crushing her back against the soft pillows. 'I only know the concept of work used to be the most important thing in my life. Now, here I am making excuses not to leave you!'

'Well, that's how it should be,' averred Holly blissfully, and Morgan did not contradict her.

ROMANCE

Variety is the spice of romance

Each month, Mills & Boon publish new romances. New stories about people falling in love. A world of variety in romance — from the best writers in the romantic world. Choose from these titles in February.

LOVE ME NOT Lindsay Armstrong
THE WINTER HEART Lillian Cheatham
DESIRE FOR REVENGE Penny Jordan
AN ALL-CONSUMING PASSION Anne Mather
KNIGHT'S POSSESSION Carole Mortimer
THE COUNTERFEIT SECRETARY Susan Napier
SUNSTROKE Elizabeth Oldfield
BEST LAID PLANS Rosemary Schneider
DANGEROUS MOONLIGHT Kay Thorpe
A MOMENT IN TIME Yvonne Whittal
***FROM THIS DAY FORWARD** Sandra Marton
***THAT MAN FROM TEXAS** Quinn Wilder

On sale where you buy paperbacks. If you require further information or have any difficulty obtaining them, write to: Mills & Boon Reader Service, PO Box 236, Thornton Road, Croydon, Surrey CR9 3RU, England.

*These two titles are available *only* from Mills & Boon Reader Service.

Mills & Boon
the rose of romance

ROMANCE

Next month's romances from Mills & Boon

Each month, you can choose from a world of variety in romance with Mills & Boon. These are the new titles to look out for next month.

RECKLESS Amanda Carpenter
MAN IN THE PARK Emma Darcy
AN UNBREAKABLE BOND Robyn Donald
ONE IN A MILLION Sandra Field
DIPLOMATIC AFFAIR Claire Harrison
POWER POINT Rowan Kirby
DARK BETRAYAL Patricia Lake
NO LONGER A DREAM Carole Mortimer
A SCARLET WOMAN Margaret Pargeter
A LASTING KIND OF LOVE Catherine Spencer
*BLUEBELLS ON THE HILL Barbara McMahon
*RETURN TO FARAWAY Valerie Parv

Buy them from your usual paperback stockist, or write to: Mills & Boon Reader Service, P.O. Box 236, Thornton Rd, Croydon, Surrey CR9 3RU, England. Readers in South Africa-write to: Mills & Boon Reader Service of Southern Africa, Private Bag X3010, Randburg, 2125.

*These two titles are available *only* from Mills & Boon Reader Service.

Mills & Boon
the rose of romance

Rebecca had set herself on course for loneliness and despair. It took a plane crash and a struggle to survive in the wilds of the Canadian Northwest Territories to make her change – and to let her fall in love with the only other survivor, handsome Guy McLaren.

Arctic Rose is her story – and you can read it from the 14th February for just £2.25.

The story continues with Rebecca's sister, Tamara, available soon.